This can't be real. . . .

Jessica looked around her. There were glowing candles and headily scented flowers all through the living room. Music played softly in the background—raunchy, sensuous blues. The table was covered with a black cloth and set for two. On one of the plates was an orchid tinted the blue-green of the sea.

This can't be real, she told herself. *I must be in a movie or a fairy tale. . . .* Mike came up behind her, cocooning her in his arms, his kisses like fireflies dancing on her skin. *Or in a dream . . .*

"I made salmon mousse to start," he whispered, the fireflies moving gently down her neck. "And chicken in wine and herbs for the entrée." The fireflies started a tango across her back. "And for dessert—"

"Maybe we can skip dessert . . ." she whispered.

Once more Mike lifted her in his arms. "Maybe we can start with it," he said.

D1144253

Bantam Books in the Sweet Valley University series:

1. COLLEGE GIRLS
2. LOVE, LIES AND JESSICA WAKEFIELD
3. WHAT YOUR PARENTS DON'T KNOW
4. ANYTHING FOR LOVE

SWEET VALLEY UNIVERSITY

Love, Lies, and Jessica Wakefield

Written by
Laurie John

Created by
FRANCINE PASCAL

BANTAM BOOKS
NEW YORK · TORONTO · LONDON · SYDNEY · AUCKLAND

For Mia Pascal Johansson

LOVE, LIES AND JESSICA WAKEFIELD
A BANTAM BOOK 0 553 40788 0

Originally published in USA by Bantam Books

First publication in Great Britain

PRINTING HISTORY
Bantam edition published 1995
Bantam edition reprinted 1995

Sweet Valley High® and Sweet Valley University™ are
trademarks of Francine Pascal.

Conceived by Francine Pascal

Produced by Daniel Weiss Associates, Inc., 33 West 17th Street,
New York, NY 10011

All rights reserved.

Copyright © 1993 by Francine Pascal
Cover art copyright © 1993 by Daniel Weiss Associates, Inc.

Conditions of Sale
1. This book is sold subject to the condition that it shall not,
by way of trade or otherwise, be lent, re-sold, hired out or
otherwise circulated without the publisher's prior consent in any
form of binding or cover other than that in which it is published
and without a similar condition including this condition being
imposed on the subsequent purchaser.
2. This book is sold subject to the Standard Conditions of Sale
of Net Books and may not be re-sold in the UK below the net price
fixed by the publishers for the book.

Bantam Books are published by Transworld Publishers Ltd,
61–63 Uxbridge Road, Ealing, London W5 5SA,
in Australia by Transworld Publishers (Australia) Pty Ltd,
15–25 Helles Avenue, Moorebank, NSW 2170,
and in New Zealand by Transworld Publishers (NZ) Ltd,
3 William Pickering Drive, Albany, Auckland.

Printed and bound in Great Britain by
Cox & Wyman Ltd, Reading, Berkshire.

Chapter One

"How can you sit there, gazing into space like that?" Isabella Ricci demanded, groaning dramatically. "It's Friday night. Gorgeous, sophisticated young college women like us are supposed to be out partying on Friday night, not sitting in their dorm twiddling their thumbs."

Does she think I don't know that? Jessica wondered. She had started her countdown to the weekend on Monday morning. But she couldn't trust herself to answer her roommate right away. She wasn't sure she could speak without bursting into tears. Here it was Friday—a night when no one even *pretended* to do any work—and she, Jessica Wakefield, was staring at a wall. As much as she liked Isabella, she was not the person Jessica wanted to be spending the evening with. The person she wanted was tall, dark, and dangerously handsome. The person she wanted was Michael

1

McAllery—but at the moment it didn't seem as though Michael McAllery wanted her.

Isabella was looking at her expectantly. "I'm not twiddling my thumbs," Jessica finally said. *I'm torturing myself,* she added silently, *wondering where he is right now*. And wondering whether or not he was alone.

"Oh, no?" Isabella raised one perfectly sculpted eyebrow. "Maybe you're right. Twiddling would be too much activity. You haven't moved at all. You've been sitting there for almost an hour, staring at the wall."

"Thinking," Jessica said by way of explanation. Much to Jessica's relief, Isabella didn't ask her *what* she was thinking. Because Isabella wouldn't have approved. Isabella didn't know much more about the enigmatic Mike McAllery than Jessica did, but insisted everything she did know was bad.

"Well, I was thinking too," Isabella said, shaking her dark, tousled hair. "I mean, what's wrong with the guys on this campus? Have aliens cut off their testosterone supply? How can two of the sexiest, most sophisticated, most desirable women at Sweet Valley University not have dates on a Friday night?"

I wish I knew, thought Jessica. *I wish I knew how he could say he'd call and just not. Not even to make up some excuse.* Her attention went back to the wall. Was it something she'd said? Something she'd done? Had he met someone he thought was prettier, sometime between Wednesday and today?

"Jessica! Are you listening to me?"

Jessica dragged her mind back to her roommate. She put on one of her best cheerleader smiles. "You could have had a date," she reminded Isabella. "In fact, you could have had two dates, if I remember correctly. Didn't that hunk on the wrestling team ask you out? And the graduate student who works in the bookstore?"

Sexy, sophisticated Isabella stuck out her tongue. "The hunk has muscles where his brains should be, and the guy in the bookstore wears mohair." She gave Jessica a critical look. "Anyway, what about you? A different guy called you every day this week."

In the past Jessica had been interested in every good-looking man she met. If three different guys had asked her out for the weekend, she would have gone out with all of them. But now there was only one man Jessica wanted to see.

"They were all dorks," Jessica said dismissively.

"You mean you didn't want to go out with any of them." Isabella's look became serious. "You'd rather sit around here waiting for the mystery man, Mike McAllery, to call."

Jessica scowled. Isabella hadn't been fooled after all. It was bad enough when Jessica's identical twin sister, Elizabeth, knew what she was thinking without being told, but having Isabella do it was too much. They weren't even related.

3

"What makes you think I'm waiting for Mike?" she asked innocently.

Isabella made a face. "Oh, give me a break, will you, Jess? Ever since he rescued you from that goon at the Halloween dance, you've been moping around like Mike McAllery's water and you're dying of thirst."

"I have not."

"Oh, yes, you have." Isabella hurled herself from the sofa. "I'm not saying I'm much better, turning down someone who looks like a body double for the Terminator just because I'm hoping Tom Watts will ask me out. But at least Tom is a nice guy. He's not a drinking, womanizing—"

"Stop it!" Jessica put her hands over her ears. "Stop it, Isabella. I mean it. I'm sick of you and my brother, Steven, trying to turn me against Mike. You're wrong about him. He's kind, and caring, and thoughtful. If you could have seen the way he handled that thug who tried to scare me you'd know that you're wrong." *If you could feel how he kisses me, you'd know you're wrong*, she added silently. She scowled at Isabella. "For all you know, Isabella, Mike's had an accident or something, and right this minute he's lying in a hospital too hurt to call and tell me what's happened."

Isabella rolled her intelligent gray eyes. "You really are too much, you know that?" She came over and sat down on the arm of Jessica's chair. "Jess," she said, her voice suddenly gentle. "I'm not trying

4

to turn you against Mike. I mean that. And neither is Steven. We're just concerned about you, that's all. Mike McAllery's out of your league. Why can't you see that? This guy's like Jesse James. He's wild and romantic, but you wouldn't want to depend on him to pick up the milk on his way home." She put a hand on Jessica's shoulder. "And anyway, if he's so caring and thoughtful, why are you sitting here waiting for the phone to ring?"

In her mind, Jessica played back the end of her last date with Mike. His arms were around her, his lips were on hers, his breath was warm against her skin. *I'll see you,* he had said. *I'll call.* She fought back the threat of tears. "He didn't say exactly when he'd call, Isabella. He is busy, you know. He's not just a college kid. He's got other things to do."

"I'm sure he does," Isabella said knowingly.

"Business," Jessica snapped, her eyes flashing.

Isabella held up her hands. "All right, all right. I don't want to fight about Mike; he's not worth it." She stood up. "What say you and I go out and get a pizza? Just because we don't have dates doesn't mean we can't go out and have a good time."

Jessica looked up at Isabella in disbelief. *Go out now? What if he calls? What if he decides to stop by?* a voice in her head was screaming.

"You go," she said calmly. "I'm not really hungry."

Isabella put her hands on her hips. "Not really hungry? Jessica, you haven't eaten anything since breakfast. Since when can't you be tempted by a pineapple pizza with two kinds of cheese?"

"No, really." Jessica yawned, not meeting Isabella's gaze. "I'm tired. It's been a long week. I just want to stay here and relax."

"Jessica," Isabella said, enunciating each syllable. "You cannot spend the rest of your life in this room, waiting for Mike to show up. You can't let him call all the shots. You have to—"

"I'm not letting him call all the shots, Isabella," Jessica cut in. "Really. I just don't feel like going out. I'm exhausted."

"Snack bar," Isabella said. "That isn't as far as the pizza parlor. You can take the phone off the hook so he thinks you're talking to someone, and leave a note on the door in case he does come by."

But what if he calls the operator and finds that the line isn't busy? What if he thinks I left the phone off the hook because I don't want to talk to him? What if he doesn't come to the door? What if he comes to the door, but the note's fallen off and he doesn't see it? What if he's insulted that I left him a note?

"Isabella, it's not because of Mike. Really. I'm just not hungry, and I don't feel like going out."

Isabella picked up her jacket from the sofa. "Okay, fine. Suit yourself. If you change your mind, I'll either be at the snack bar or at Vito's."

Jessica kept her eyes straight ahead as Isabella walked past her. "I won't change my mind."

Isabella stopped at the door and looked back.

6

"No," she said with a sigh. "I don't think you will."

Elizabeth and Jessica Wakefield might have looked identical, with their blue-green eyes and their long blond hair, but that was where the resemblance ended. Inside, the twins couldn't have been more unalike. Jessica had always been the frivolous, fun-loving sister, and Elizabeth had always been the hardworking and dependable one.

Which is why Jessica is probably at some wild party being asked out by twenty-five different guys, and I'm headed to the library to finish my English paper, Elizabeth thought as she pulled a baggy black hooded sweatshirt over her Save Our Planet T-shirt. She knew that everybody else in the world had a date or a party to go to that night and that she'd probably be the only person in the library, but she didn't want to stay in her room. Even though Celine Boudreaux, Elizabeth's roommate, wouldn't be back for hours, Elizabeth disliked Celine so much that she spent as much time out of the room as she could. Just the smell of Celine's perfume and the sight of her clothes thrown all over were enough to make Elizabeth's blood pressure rise.

As she turned from her desk, Elizabeth caught a glimpse of herself in the mirror. Recently, a new difference between her and her sister had appeared. Now only one of the Wakefield twins was a perfect size six, and it wasn't Elizabeth.

The truth was, she'd been having a difficult

time adjusting to college life. Not only did she have to live with Celine, the Scarlett O'Hara of SVU, who had come all the way from Louisiana just to make Elizabeth's life miserable, but in just the first few weeks of school she'd broken up with her long-standing boyfriend, Todd Wilkins, and had grown apart from both her sister and her best friend, Enid Rollins. It seemed as if the only thing she hadn't lost was her appetite.

"That's what you get for turning to food for comfort," Elizabeth told her reflection, giving a tug at the tight waistband of her jeans. "Discomfort."

Her stomach growled.

"No," she told it. "You're on a diet. You've had your fifteen hundred calories for today, and that's all you're getting."

Her stomach gave another plaintive rumble. Not that Elizabeth blamed it. Ever since she had started this diet, she was hungry all the time. The funny thing was that even though she hadn't cheated once, she didn't seem to be losing any weight. The book she was using said it was because she was on a plateau, but to Elizabeth it felt more like a valley.

Her eyes fell on the open bag of nacho chips on Celine's bed. Celine could stuff her face with junk food from morning till night and never gain an ounce. It was just another thing to hold against her. Elizabeth's stomach moaned.

"Library!" Elizabeth commanded, snapping off the light and practically fleeing the room.

Nonetheless, as she marched purposefully across campus, Elizabeth's mind was not on the nineteenth-century British novel, where it was supposed to be. It was on food. Everything she saw made her hungry. Soda cans, candy wrappers, a pizza box, even a poster outside the new arts complex advertising a performance of *The Cherry Orchard* by the student theater group.

At the edge of the quad she froze. There, coming toward her from the other side, was her ex-best friend, Enid Rollins, eating what looked suspiciously like a burrito grande.

This was the one time since they had arrived at the university that Elizabeth wished Enid would just walk right by her. *Please don't stop*, she silently prayed. *Be in a hurry. Don't see me.*

"Hi, Liz!"

Enid stopped close enough for Elizabeth to see that it was a jumbo chicken burrito with guacamole and sour cream.

"Hi, Enid."

Enid sighed. "Alex, Liz, not Enid. How many times do I have to tell you? It's like you have this pathological—"

"I'm sorry, Alex," she apologized quickly. The last thing Elizabeth needed was a half-hour lecture on Enid's new name while she watched her eat. "My mind was somewhere else." Most of the time she did manage to remember that Enid wanted to be called Alex or Alexandra now that she was at college and had a new image, but the burrito had made her forget. There was salsa on it besides the guacamole and the sour cream. Enid took another bite. And melted cheese.

Chewing slowly, Enid nodded at the books in Elizabeth's arms. "Where are you going? Don't tell me you're studying tonight."

Enid used to be the person Elizabeth told everything to. She was the one person to whom Elizabeth could have admitted how miserable she was, and that the only things she liked about college were her classes and her apprenticeship at the TV station. But things had changed so much between them since they arrived that she couldn't bring herself to tell Enid the truth: that she was working on a Friday night because she had nothing else to do.

"I've got an English paper due on Monday," Elizabeth said with a groan. "The professor's a real tyrant. I think he must have been Louis the Fourteenth in a former life."

Enid laughed. "My sociology teacher's like that. We're all afraid to breathe too loud."

Elizabeth sighed with relief as Enid swallowed the last of her burrito. "So, what are you doing on your own on a Friday night?" she asked. "I thought you'd be out with Mark."

Enid had been dating campus basketball star

Mark Gathers, a friend of Todd's, almost since school started. They were already quite an item.

"I thought so too." Enid made a face. "But you know those jocks. There's always somebody wanting to give them a dinner or take them out or something." She giggled. "It's a good thing he gets the grades he needs without having to work too hard, because with practice and everything he doesn't have that much time left to study."

Elizabeth felt a pang that wasn't hunger. She used to know exactly what those jocks were like, but she hadn't seen Todd in weeks. Occasionally she'd catch a glimpse of him, striding across the campus like a young god, and once again feel amazed that someone she had been so close to could now be so far away.

Enid didn't seem to notice that she was upset. "The way athletes are treated on the campus really is unbelievable, isn't it?" Enid continued. "Sometimes after a game I have to wait forever before Mark can get away from his admirers to take me out." She made another face, but Elizabeth could tell that Enid was secretly proud to be the girlfriend of one of the biggest jocks at school.

Elizabeth used to know what that felt like. She felt another pang sear her heart.

"Well," she said, already starting to move forward. "I'd better get to work or I'll be up all night."

Enid nodded. "Right. I've got to go too. Mark's picking me up for a late date after his dinner, so I want to get a nap before then. I'll see you around, Liz."

"Sure," Elizabeth called over her shoulder. "I'll see you around."

That's the one good thing about having someone turn a knife in your heart, Elizabeth told herself as she raced up the library steps. *It makes you forget all about your stomach for a while.*

Danny Wyatt's heavy footsteps echoed as he walked down the corridor of the campus television station. During the day and on weekends there was always a lot of activity in the WSVU offices—camerapeople, soundpeople, and reporters running in and out, everyone shouting and behind schedule—but on a Friday night there would be only one or two people in the studio, running music videos of local bands.

Danny made a left turn into a silent, empty hall. There *should* have been only one or two people in the studio, but Danny had a hunch that he might find an extra person in the newsroom, working overtime as usual.

Danny stopped at the door marked NEWS, and listened. Nothing, not even the faintest of sounds. *I know he's in there,* Danny told himself. Shaking his head, he opened the door without knocking.

The room was dark and the desks were empty—except for the desk in the farthest corner, where a light was shining and a tall, broad, dark-haired young man was hunched over, reading so intently that he didn't even look up when Danny shut the door behind him.

"Hey, what a surprise."

Without turning around, Tom Watts held up one finger. "Hold on," he ordered. "I've just gotten to the good part."

Danny came up behind him. "What are you doing, man? It's Friday night. Nobody works this late on a Friday night." He put a hand on his roommate's shoulder. "And besides, I've been waiting for you for two hours. We were supposed to play some tennis tonight and go out for Thai food."

"I don't feel like playing tennis," Tom said. His eyes didn't move from the page he was reading.

Danny laughed. "Well, neither do I. *Anymore*. But I do feel like eating. Or has your reporter's brain cut off all communication to your stomach again?"

"This is incredible, Danny. Really incredible. If half of this is true, we're really onto something here."

"What is it? More on the Halloween hoax?"

A few weeks before Halloween, a local psychic had predicted that a psychopath would make an appearance at the university's Halloween dance. Rumors had built up to an almost hysterical pitch. Like the good investigative reporter he was, Tom had set about interviewing everyone from faculty

13

and students to the psychic himself, following his own instincts. In the end, there had been two unpleasant events at the dance—one a racial incident involving Danny and the other an attack on Jessica Wakefield. Tom was not only sure that the attack on Jessica had been meant for her sister, he was also sure that Peter Wilbourne III, president of the Sigmas, the most prestigious fraternity on campus, was behind both. Tom had been working on a follow-up ever since.

Tom shook his head. "No, I still haven't found anything solid on Wilbourne. This is something completely different. Something I stumbled on by accident."

Danny leaned over Tom's shoulder, his eyes scanning the typed page. It was a letter to the co-captain of the basketball team, canceling repayment on a student loan. When he got to the bottom, Danny whistled. "This is dynamite, Tombo. They let Howser borrow five thousand dollars to top off his scholarship and then they just let him have the money because he's so valuable to the team." He whistled again. "They never did anything like that for me when I was on the wrestling team."

Tom laughed. "They never did anything like that for me when I was their star quarterback, either. But then, they didn't have to work hard to recruit me." He took two more pieces of paper from his desk and handed them to Danny.

"Marotta's grade transcripts," Danny said. Marotta was Tom's replacement on the football team.

Tom leaned back and spun his chair around so he was facing his friend. "Look at them closely."

Danny frowned, puzzled. "One semester he was flunking everything, and the other he was doing C's and B's."

Tom gave him a slow smile. "Look again, amigo."

"I don't believe it." Danny's eyes moved from one paper to the other. "They're for the same semester."

"That's right." Tom's voice was tight with excitement. "Obviously somebody was supposed to throw out the first transcript, only they forgot."

Danny stared back at him in amazement. "But how did you get hold of it?"

"Pure chance. I just happened to be in the athletics office, doing some background on the basketball team for a special we're doing on the new season, and I found the letter about the loan mixed in with some clippings and stuff like that. At first I didn't think anything of it. I mean, I thought it was strange, but I figured there was something I didn't know. Like, maybe somebody else, some alumnus for instance, had paid off the loan. Then all of a sudden I thought of Marotta." Tom grinned. "Not only isn't he as good a quarterback as I was, but he isn't as smart, either. And I remembered there was a lot of talk about whether or not he'd be able to keep up his average. So I just thought I'd look in his file while I was there. You know, see how he was doing."

Danny laughed. "Remind me not to leave anything unlocked around you." He nodded at the other papers on the desk. "What else have you got?"

"Not much, really." Tom shrugged. "I've got a letter from a kid who went somewhere else, thanking the coach for bringing him out here from New York to see the school and putting up him and his family. And I've got a picture of the captain of the basketball team riding around Florida in a rented Porsche when they went there to play Miami. And I've got some notes of my own about how the jocks are housed and stuff like that. It's all pretty much hunches and supposition, but I think the pieces are going to fit."

"So what happens next? You don't sleep or eat for the next three weeks? I forget I have a roommate?"

Tom laughed. "I'm afraid you're out of luck this time, man. I'm not going to be able to do the digging on this one. I'm too well known, especially in the athletics department. As it was, Coach Sanchez was looking at me funny when I left. If I start hanging around there, he'll know something's up."

Danny gave his best friend a skeptical look. "You're not trying to tell me that you're going to forget about this, are you?"

"Are you nuts? Forget about this?" Tom laughed. "No, someone else is going to get the story. I'll just be the presenter."

"Who?" Danny asked, not hiding his surprise. "You're not exactly a born delegator, Tom. You never trust anybody else to do anything."

Tom turned back to the desk, locking the papers in his top drawer. "There's one person I trust enough," he said over his shoulder.

Danny stared at his back. "Who?"

"Elizabeth."

Tom's voice was so low and so fast that Danny wasn't sure he'd heard him right. "Elizabeth? You mean Elizabeth Wakefield?"

"Yeah." Tom glanced over at him. "You know I'm training her to work at the station."

Danny continued to stare. "And you know that her boyfriend is one of the big jocks on the basketball team."

Something locked in Tom's dark eyes. "Ex-boyfriend."

Danny knew that there was something going on with Tom, something concerning Elizabeth Wakefield. But he also knew that Tom wasn't going to tell him what it was. Not without a struggle. Tom was the best friend Danny had ever had, but not because they talked a lot. He kept his own counsel, just as Danny did.

"Right," Danny said calmly. "Ex-boyfriend." He grinned. "So, does that mean we can eat?"

Elizabeth spent so much time in the library that by now she usually found a few familiar—even

17

friendly—faces in the study carrels. Tom Watts, Elizabeth's boss at the TV station, was often there, working late. So was Nina Harper, who lived on her floor in Dickenson Hall. She seemed to be one of the few girls on their hall who hadn't completely fallen under Celine's spell. And then there was the coolly handsome blond man with the glacier eyes, William White. At least two or three times a week Elizabeth found him sitting at the back when she arrived, watching her as though he'd been waiting just for her.

But none of them were in the library tonight. The only students bent over the desks were people who, like Elizabeth, obviously had nothing else to do. The losers of Sweet Valley U.

Stop feeling sorry for yourself, Elizabeth scolded, trying to concentrate on what H. F. Mullerman had to say about the wit and irony of Jane Austen. But she couldn't stop feeling sorry for herself. Meeting Enid had upset her too much.

Elizabeth stared blankly at the page in front of her. It wasn't really meeting Enid that had upset her. She was relieved that she and Enid were at least speaking again. It was because talking about superjocks and the basketball team made her start thinking about Todd again.

Sometimes Elizabeth almost thought that she was over the breakup. It had been her decision as much as his. Todd had wanted to take their relationship further than she was prepared to go. He seemed

18

to think that now that he was a Big Man on Campus, Elizabeth should automatically want to sleep with him, but Elizabeth hadn't wanted to. She'd wanted to get used to her new world, with all its new experiences and feelings, before she made a commitment like that. A vision of Todd and her, holding each other as they were in the photograph she kept on her bureau, covered the page of Professor Mullerman's flawless prose. Elizabeth sniffed back a wayward tear. Sometimes she thought she was over him, and other times she knew she wasn't.

Unable to concentrate, Elizabeth checked her watch. It was getting late, but not late enough to go back to the dorm. Elizabeth couldn't do that until she was sure that she'd fall asleep right away. The last thing she wanted was to be awake when Celine got back. Celine sober in the middle of the day was bad enough, but Celine after she'd been partying all night was unbearable. They almost always wound up having a fight.

It was an off-campus party, filled with loud music, laughter, and handsome men, but still Celine Boudreaux was bored.

Idly playing with the miniature white rose she'd taken from the vase beside her, she stared back at the very attractive but exhaustingly dull young man in front of her. His name was either Darren or Daryl and he was a philosophy major. For some reason he was trying to seduce her by explaining

Aristotle's ethics to her. Celine wasn't interested in anybody's ethics. Ethics were like rules: they cramped your style.

"Excuse me," she said in her soft, sexy drawl. "But I just want to go refill my glass."

Even though he'd been in the middle of a sentence, he smiled back at her.

That was the advantage of having a Southern accent among Yankees. No matter what you said, they thought it must be something nice.

Without a backward glance Celine floated out of the room, her perfume drifting behind her like a train of blossoms. She could feel the eyes on her. Celine considered her granny to be a first-class witch in many ways, but she had to admit that her granny often gave good advice. Always make an entrance and always make an exit, her granny had told her. And that's what Celine always did.

Coming into the kitchen, she caught her reflection in the window over the counter. *You look gorgeous,* she told herself, pouring another drink. *You look stunningly, devastatingly, eat-your-heart-out gorgeous.*

Behind her, in the window, she could see other reflections. There was a drippy guy from her English class and Nina Something from her hall.

And suddenly there appeared someone she'd been looking for all night. The reflection showed a young man wearing an expensive black linen suit.

20

He was as beautiful as a fairy-tale prince. And he looked as bored as she felt.

A shadow crossed Celine's heart. She was extremely good at manipulating people. There were very few people she couldn't get around. One was her ghastly roommate, Elizabeth Little Goody Two-Shoes Wakefield. And the other was standing behind her, talking to a guy who looked as if one of his parents must have been a tank.

Celine took a deep breath and swung slowly around. She was also good at getting what she wanted. And she wanted the young man in black like she had never wanted anyone—if only because he didn't want her.

"William!" she gushed, gracefully sliding between him and the tank and tapping the flower against his chest. "I didn't know you were here. What a nice surprise!"

He looked from her to the rose. For just a second the bored expression in his eyes was replaced with something else: disdain. Then he took the flower from her hand and went on talking as though she weren't there. He sounded just a little bit drunk.

"It sounds to me like your friend went to the wrong part of Mexico," he said to the tank. "It's too bad you didn't tell me he was going. I could have recommended an incredible beach."

Celine's smile grew brighter. "Oh, Mexico." She sighed. "I love Mexico. Isn't it just the most romantic place?"

21

William continued to ignore her, but the tank began to speak. "Um . . . uh . . . William," he said, his eyes on Celine. "I don't believe I've met your friend."

William looked at him blankly. "My friend?"

It was at times like these that Celine wished her granny were a real witch. If she were, Celine would be able to put a spell on William White that would destroy his happiness for the rest of his life.

She turned toward the tank. "Celine," she said, her voice as soft as velvet and as sweet as pecan pie. "Celine Boudreaux."

The tank grabbed her hand so roughly she thought he was going to shake it loose from her wrist. "I'm glad to meet you, Celine," he said. He sounded glad. "I've been wanting to meet you since the beginning of the year. I'm Steve Hawkins." He grinned at her mindlessly. "I've seen you around."

Well, I haven't seen you. She looked down for a second, so he would think she was blushing modestly. *And if I had, I would've run.*

"You mean you noticed me?" she whispered. "You noticed little me in a school this big?"

Impossible though it seemed, the grin became even more mindless. "I'd notice you anywhere."

"Did you hear that, William? Your friend's been wanting to meet me." Celine glanced over her shoulder.

William White was gone.

Celine stared at the space where William had

been, her pretty mouth set in a smile as hard as industrial steel. The fact that she hadn't been able to turn William White into a horned toad or a hunchback with black teeth and b.o. wasn't really important. She was going to destroy his happiness anyway. Totally and completely. It was just going to take her a little longer to do without the help of witchcraft, that was all.

Elizabeth pushed her notebook aside with a sigh. Maybe she'd just lean back and close her eyes for a few minutes, try to re-energize herself. All she needed was to relax a little. From somewhere behind her cellophane crackled.

Her eyes snapped open. *I don't believe this. Somebody's eating!* If it wasn't her broken heart that was giving her a hard time, it was her stomach. She was sure she could smell garlic-and-onion potato chips.

This is really unfair, she said to herself. *You're not supposed to eat in the library. It's against the rules.* There was another crackle of a wrapper being torn, this one from the other side of the aisle. Now she was sure she could smell chocolate. The only thing that could make this moment worse would be if Todd Wilkins walked in right now with another girl on his arm and a cheeseburger in his hand.

I'm not going to be able to put up with this. I'll have to go get a cup of coffee. Elizabeth started gathering her things.

"I knew I'd find you here."

Every thought in Elizabeth's head drained away. She had never heard that voice before—not this close, not speaking to her—but she knew before she raised her eyes whose voice it was. She looked up to find herself staring into a pair of blue eyes so light they looked like ice.

He had a smile that was as secretive as it was dazzling. Elizabeth could never decide whether she thought the secrets it hid were good or bad.

He leaned against the carrel. His eyes might be cool, but his breath was warm. Warm and smelling faintly of wine.

"Tell me one thing," he whispered. "What's someone like you doing in the library on a night shot through with stars?"

She said the first thing that came to her mind. The truth. "Jane Austen."

"Well, I certainly wouldn't want to deprive Jane Austen of your company." He lifted his hand. "But I got this for you."

Elizabeth took the delicate white flower and sat there staring at it for several seconds, not quite knowing what to say. When she looked up again, William White was gone.

Chapter Two

Jessica opened the door to her twin's room with uncharacteristic caution, standing in the entrance for a second and looking around. Elizabeth was sitting at her desk with her back to her, her head bent over something she was writing.

Leave it to Liz, thought Jessica in exasperation. *Forty-five minutes till the big Theta tea and my sister's studying. It's a good thing she isn't Cinderella. She'd be too busy finishing her English assignment to get to the ball.*

"Psst . . ." she called in an exaggerated whisper. "Where's the South's Revenge?" Jessica was one of the few people in the world who hadn't been fooled by the charm Celine used to fool everyone else. The first time Jessica met her sister's roommate, Celine had mistaken her for Elizabeth and treated her viciously.

Elizabeth looked up and smiled. "It's okay, Jess.

Celine's out shopping." Elizabeth glanced meaningfully at the heaps of clothes around the room and at Celine's closet, crammed so full that the door wouldn't close. "Apparently she has nothing to wear to the Homecoming dance."

Jessica, who also had a room heaped with clothes, a bulging closet, and nothing to wear to the Homecoming dance, made no comment. Instead she gave her sister a stern look and shut the door behind her. She crossed the room and sat on Elizabeth's bed.

"Why aren't you dressed yet?" she demanded. "We have to be at the Theta house by three o'clock. *Today.*"

Elizabeth chewed on the top of her pen. "To tell you the truth, Jess, I'm not so sure I want to go."

"You what?" Jessica gazed at her sister in disbelief. How could they have come from a single egg and have so little in common? "What are you talking about, Elizabeth? This is the last Theta rush event. This is where they start to make their final decisions on pledges. You *have* to go."

"Not if I don't want to join their sorority, I don't," Elizabeth answered.

"*Not* join Theta?" Jessica squealed. "Elizabeth Wakefield, have you completely lost your mind? Theta was Mom's sorority. It's practically thanks to her that it's the most important sorority on campus today. Mom's a legend there, Liz. You not joining would be like Prince Charles of England deciding to move to Detroit and work at the Ford plant."

Elizabeth gave her one of her tolerant smiles. "I know it was Mom's sorority, Jess, but I'm not really sure it's right for me." She pushed her chair away from the desk. "If I do join a sorority, I think I'd like to join the Pi Beta Phis."

Now Jessica knew for sure that she and Elizabeth weren't really related at all. It was obviously some sort of weird cosmic accident that they looked exactly alike, had the same parents, and had been raised in the same house.

"The Pi Beta Phis?" Jessica screeched. "*You* want to join the Pis?" She sat up, leaning forward earnestly. "Elizabeth, nobody who wants a social life at SVU joins the Pis. The Pis eat soy burgers and crusade to save South American tree toads. They think a party is sitting around singing *Guantanamera!* while some girl who's never heard of makeup plays the guitar. They do nothing but study and take up causes, Liz. They're boring. They're dull and—" The words froze on Jessica's lips. The more she described the Pis, the more obvious it was that they were just like her sister. Boring. Dull. More interested in studying and recycling their bottles than in having fun.

"You mean they're just like me?" Elizabeth asked, but she was smiling and there was a humorous glint in her eye.

Jessica got up suddenly, grabbing her sister's hand and pulling her to her feet. "But you don't have to be dull and boring, Liz," she said sincerely.

"You could be one of the most popular girls on campus if you just tried a little harder. After all"—she smiled brightly—"you look exactly like me."

"But Jessica—" Elizabeth protested as Jessica dragged her over to her closet. "Maybe I don't want to be one of the most popular girls on campus anymore. Maybe I think other things are more important."

Jessica gave Elizabeth a "you would" look and opened her closet. She was determined that this was one argument she was going to win. After all, you never could tell about sorority politics. If Elizabeth turned down the Thetas, they might turn down Jessica. Or—worse yet—if the Thetas realized how dull and boring Elizabeth really was, they might think Jessica was the same way.

Jessica rummaged through Elizabeth's clothes, looking for something sophisticated enough for the Theta tea. She finally pulled out a slinky pink sheath and held it up to her twin. "You owe me this," she informed her sister. "You owe it to Mom. You were born to be a Theta, Liz, and that's all there is to it." She shoved the dress into Elizabeth's hands. "Here. Put this on."

Reluctantly Elizabeth got out of her jeans and T-shirt and put on the dress.

Something was wrong. Jessica took a step backward, eyeing her sister critically. She remembered when Elizabeth bought this dress, because she'd bought one just like it. They'd caused quite a sensation at the spring fling last year. Everyone had said they looked like models. She took another step back. Elizabeth didn't look like a model in this dress anymore; she looked like a sausage.

Elizabeth turned to the mirror. "Really, Jessica. I don't feel comfortable in this dress. I'd rather wear something more casual."

You mean you'd rather wear something bigger, Jessica thought, realizing that her sister had not only become more boring since she'd arrived at college but that she'd put on weight as well. A strange, unpleasant sensation crawled through Jessica's heart. She and Elizabeth had always been different, but they'd always looked the same, and they'd always been close. All at once the differences between them seemed enormous. Elizabeth wasn't just like her. Not anymore.

"I have that nice peasant skirt," Elizabeth said. "I could wear that with my—"

"Give me a break, will you, Liz?" Jessica said. "You can't dress like a peasant for the Theta pledge tea." She put her arm around Elizabeth and smiled at their reflection. For the first time in eighteen years they didn't look completely identical.

It was a perfect California Saturday afternoon. The sky was blue, the air was warm, and the sun was shining. Everyone was outside—playing softball, riding bikes, or just lying in the sun on the beach. Everyone, that was, except Winston Egbert.

Winston was lying under his bed in Oakley Hall, trying not to breathe too loudly. Outside his room, three of his Sigma pals, Bill Montana, Tony Calavieri, and Jeff Cross, were pounding on the door.

Winston groaned silently. Ever since the Sigmas had discovered that Winston was the only male living in an all-girl dorm, they wouldn't leave him alone. They were always dropping by, or taking him out, or following him around, hoping he'd introduce them to girls. Winston had enjoyed this newfound popularity at first, but he was getting tired of it.

And the Sigmas were making it hard for him to get a date himself. The only time he could talk to a girl without some Sigma suddenly looming over her shoulder was when he was in the Oakley Hall bathroom. Winston groaned again as he imagined asking Denise Waters, the most fantastic girl in the entire world, to go out with him. "What about Saturday night? I thought we could hang out in the bathroom for a couple of hours."

Winston checked his watch again. It was two thirty, two thirty on a Saturday afternoon. Somewhere on the SVU campus there was a softball game with his name on it. Winston's stomach growled. Somewhere in the SVU snack bar there was a double chili cheeseburger wondering where he was.

The door shook as the Sigmas started knocking again. "Yo, Win!" called a voice Winston recognized as Bill's. "Win, are you in there?"

Go away! Winston yelled silently. *What are you, stupid or something? Can't you see I'm not here?*

The banging stopped suddenly.

Winston's heart did a double flip of joy. They'd given up. They'd given up and gone away.

The door opened. From beneath the hem of the bedspread, Winston could see three pairs of Nikes enter the room. His heart froze in mid-flip.

"I guess he's not here," Bill said.

Winston choked back a sigh and closed his eyes. Bill was one of the most popular guys in the fraternity, but it wasn't because he was smart.

"Where do you think he went?" Tony asked.

"Maybe he had to go into town for something," Bill suggested.

"His Beetle's outside," Jeff said.

"Maybe he got a lift with someone," said Tony.

"Can I help you guys?"

Winston opened his eyes. A fourth pair of feet, these in black-and-red cowboy boots, had appeared in the doorway. It was Maia, the dorm monitor of Oakley Hall. Winston felt like kissing the mattress. Maia was tougher than the entire NFL put together. She'd get rid of them.

"We were looking for Winston," Bill said, putting on the smooth, ingratiating voice he always used when he was near a pretty girl.

But his charm was lost on Maia. "Winnie's not here," she said shortly. "And in the future I'd ap-

31

preciate it if you were a little more quiet when you looked for him. Some people are trying to study."

The Nikes started to shuffle toward the door.

"Sure," Tony said.

"We're really sorry we disturbed you," Jeff said.

"You busy tonight?" Bill asked.

"I'll tell Winnie you dropped by," Maia said.

Very slowly and very carefully, Winston lifted the bedspread and peered out.

"Maia!" he hissed. "Are they gone?"

Maia, just about to close the door behind her, turned around. "Winnie!" She seemed surprised to see him crawling out from under the bed. "What are you doing under there?"

"What do you think I was doing?" He pulled himself to a sitting position. "I was hiding from those guys."

Maia's surprise was replaced by amusement. "But I thought you loved them. I thought your only wish in life was to be pledged to the Sigmas and be a big man on campus."

"You didn't read enough fairy tales when you were a kid," Winston said, brushing dust balls from his hair. "Or you'd realize that every wish comes with a curse."

A high, familiar laugh bounced across the room. Elizabeth looked over to the circle of giggling Thetas with her sister at the center of it. All of them were so fashionably dressed that they could have been models posing for an ad. And all of them were stuffing cake and cookies into their mouths as though they might not eat again for a week.

How is it they can eat without gaining weight and I can't? Elizabeth wondered as she sipped her cup of black tea.

Elizabeth sighed, checking her watch for the third time in the last half hour. To make Jessica happy, Elizabeth had agreed to come to the Theta tea and to wear the uncomfortable pink dress. To make Jessica happy, she'd been making an effort to be sociable and outgoing, even though most of the sorority sisters were so superficial and snobby that it was almost impossible to find anything to talk about. In the hour that she'd been here, Elizabeth had said just about all there was to say about the weather and its effects on the skin and hair, and the importance of accessories in getting the most out of your wardrobe. Elizabeth stifled a yawn. But she couldn't pretend to be having a good time, not even to make Jessica happy.

Elizabeth's thoughts were interrupted by an oily voice right behind her.

"I can't believe it," the voice was saying. "I mean, I knew you and Jessica must be related, but I never realized you were supposed to be twins! Identical twins!"

Elizabeth turned around. The owner of the oily voice was a tall brunette, so astoundingly immaculate she looked as though her clothes had been

33

washed and ironed on her body. Elizabeth recognized her immediately. She was Alison Quinn, vice president of the Thetas.

Elizabeth put a smile on her face as insincere as the one on Alison's. "We're not only supposed to be identical twins," she said sweetly. "We *are* identical twins. You can ask our mother."

If Alison noticed the sarcasm in Elizabeth's voice, she did an excellent job of disguising it. "Well, you could have fooled me," she said. Her gray eyes narrowed. "I guess it's because you have such different personalities." Alison nodded toward Jessica as a fresh wave of laughter rolled across the room. "Jessica's so outgoing . . . so gregarious . . . so—"

"Much fun," Elizabeth filled in.

"Exactly." Alison showed her perfect teeth. "Though, of course, I'm not suggesting that just because a person's quiet she can't be interesting or exciting." She looked as though she were about to yawn.

Elizabeth tightened her grip on her teacup. Would her mother and sister ever forgive her if she threw her cold tea down the front of Alison Quinn's champagne-colored silk blouse?

"Of course, you're not always so quiet, are you?" Alison went on. "You were pretty outspoken the night of the Theta-Sigma house party, if I remember right."

"You remember right," Elizabeth replied.

The joint Theta-Sigma party had been one of

the first big social events at school. Elizabeth had gone alone, and Jessica had gone with Danny Wyatt. Peter Wilbourne III, the smug, self-opinionated president of the Sigmas, was angry that Jessica had gone with Danny rather than with him, and had made a racial attack on Danny. Only the intervention of Tom Watts had stopped Peter from actually trying to rough Danny up.

After Jessica and Danny had left the party, Elizabeth had gone up to Peter Wilbourne and told him exactly what she thought of him and his fraternity. It didn't surprise her that the Thetas hadn't forgotten the incident. What surprised her was that they were still willing to consider her as a pledge. The name Alice Wakefield must have even more influence with them than Elizabeth had thought.

"Still," Alison said, her voice edged with barbed wire, "I'm sure you didn't realize what you were doing at the time, publicly attacking someone like Peter."

Elizabeth put down her cup.

"And I'm sure you're really very interesting," Alison added, sounding bored.

Elizabeth gave the Theta vice president her most dazzling smile. "You're wrong," she said, her voice as pleasant as the afternoon outside. "I *did* realize what I was doing, and I'm not very interesting at all."

Jessica had given Elizabeth an accusing look when she caught her leaving the pledge tea early, but Elizabeth didn't really care. She couldn't have stood one more minute of Alison Quinn and her sorority sisters.

As she strode across the campus, Elizabeth couldn't help smiling to herself. A few weeks ago an afternoon like the one she'd just spent would have depressed her and made her feel totally inadequate. She would probably have skulked back to the dorm and eaten half a box of cookies. Now it had just made her feel angry. She smiled again. But she still wouldn't mind at least a quarter of a box of cookies right now.

"Let Jessica live her life the way she wants, and I'll live mine the way I want," Elizabeth told herself as she marched down an unfamiliar path. She'd decided to try a shortcut because she couldn't wait to get back to her room to take off the stupid pink dress.

"There isn't anything wrong with me just because I don't want to fit in with people like that," Elizabeth said as she kicked a stone down the path in front of her. "They're wrong for acting as if everyone *should* be like them."

Elizabeth slowed as she came to an outdoor basketball court where a group of shouting, whooping guys were playing a fast pickup game. She hadn't changed so much that the sight of a basketball game didn't make her think of Todd. She still had trouble believing she'd really lost him.

Elizabeth stopped before she reached the court. The guys were all tensely watching the basket. The ball was balancing precariously on the rim, threatening to fall back to the ground. Suddenly it fell through the net. One voice stood out above the general roar that followed. "Way to go!" it shouted.

Elizabeth felt her blood turn to ice water. Todd. That was Todd's voice. Yes, there he was, wearing his old blue sweatpants and a white T-shirt soaked with sweat. His hair was damp and his face was flushed. How many times had he rushed up to her after a game, looking just like that, and taken her into his arms? Too many times. Even from here she knew exactly what he smelled like at this moment; the thought of it made her feel weak.

Elizabeth watched Todd as he darted and wove across the court, his movements quick and supple. She couldn't seem to take her eyes off him. She couldn't seem to stop her heart from pounding. Elizabeth wiped her moist palms on her dress.

When Todd had wanted her to sleep with him, she'd told him she wasn't ready.

Maybe I'm changing even more than I thought, Elizabeth told herself as she reluctantly turned away from the game before anyone saw her. *Because I certainly feel ready now.*

Enid had been so lost in her thoughts of the Theta tea and what a great time she'd had that she hadn't realized at first who the figure rushing away from the basketball court was.

"Liz!" Enid called. She hadn't even seen Elizabeth leave the sorority house. One minute Elizabeth had been there, talking to Alison Quinn, and the next she was gone. "Liz!" But Elizabeth was already out of sight.

Enid laughed, remembering what she'd heard about the scene at the Theta-Sigma party when Elizabeth told Peter Wilbourne off. Elizabeth seemed to be making a habit of leaving places abruptly lately.

"Alex! Over here!"

Instantly forgetting all about Elizabeth, Enid looked toward the court. Her boyfriend, Mark Gathers, was jogging toward her, a smile on his handsome face.

"I was beginning to worry that you weren't coming," he said as she ran to him. "I was afraid one of those Sigma creeps the Thetas hang out with had stolen you away."

Mark's clothes were wet and rivulets of sweat ran down his face, but she didn't hesitate for a second. She threw herself into his arms for a long, deep kiss.

"It would take an army of Sigmas to steal me away from you," she whispered when they finally pulled apart.

"It better," he said. He brushed a strand of hair away from her face. "So, how was it? You have a good time?"

Enid nodded. "It was terrific. They're such a great bunch of girls." She leaned against him as he wrapped his arm around her waist. "And it's unofficial, of course, but I'm definitely going to be pledged. Magda Helperin, the president, told me herself."

Mark gave her another hug. "In that case, Ms. Rollins, I think we should go out tonight for a special celebratory dinner. Just you and me, a quiet corner table at Da Vinci's, a candle, and one red rose."

She couldn't hide her surprise. "Da Vinci's? You can't be serious. Da Vinci's is the most expensive restaurant in town."

"My grant's just come through," he said, smiling at her worry. "You can even have two desserts."

She hugged him back, but then the worried look returned. "Oh, no . . ." she wailed. "We can't go out tonight. You have a big physics test on Monday, remember? You said yourself you can't afford to do badly on it."

"Don't you worry about me." He winked. "I'm a superjock, right? I'll be fine."

Enid frowned. "But I don't want to distract you from—"

He put a finger to her lips. "No buts, Alex. You don't distract me; you make me concentrate. And what I want to concentrate on is you."

I can't believe how perfect my life is, Enid thought, holding tightly to Mark's hand. *It's almost too good to be true.*

Mark turned back toward the court as they started to walk away. "See you later," he called.

"See you later," one of the other players called back.

At the sound of the other guy's voice Enid turned too. It was Todd. She'd been so glad to see Mark she hadn't even noticed Todd. That was why Elizabeth was watching the game when Enid arrived. And why she left so abruptly.

It's too bad everyone's life can't be perfect, Enid thought as she and Mark headed back to his dorm.

Cheddar-cheese potato chips, an insistent little voice was whispering in Elizabeth's head. *Forget about the Thetas. Forget about Todd. What you want are cheddar-cheese potato chips. They sell them in the snack machine in the common room. You can buy two bags.* Against her will, Elizabeth imagined locking herself in her room, closing the curtains, and snuggling up on her bed with a bag of cheddar-cheese potato chips and a good book, safe and far away from sorority teas and a sweaty man who used to call her his. It was such a comforting image that she could practically taste the salt on her lips.

Elizabeth quickened her pace as she caught sight of Dickenson Hall, rising in front of her like a desert oasis. Potato chips or no potato chips, all she wanted was to get inside.

"Elizabeth! Wait up!"

If it had been anyone else, Elizabeth would have kept on walking, but she recognized the voice immediately and stopped. It was Tom Watts. She turned around. He had a smile on his face that made the day look dull.

"How can you walk so fast in that dress and those shoes?" Tom asked, falling into step beside her.

For the first time all afternoon, Elizabeth found herself laughing. "It's genetic," she told him. "Boys get the Y chromosome and facial hair, and girls get two X chromosomes and the ability to run in heels and clothes as tight as a bandage."

He looked her up and down. "So, where have you been? Some sort of masquerade party?"

Not even an hour ago laughing seemed like the last thing she would do today, but here she was doing it again. "Is that your diplomatic way of telling me you hate my dress?"

"No, I don't *hate* your dress." He looked over at her as they walked along. "I just don't think it's very . . . uh . . . you." His voice went almost to a whisper as he added, "I like the stuff you usually wear."

Elizabeth felt herself blushing and turned away. "I guess I don't have to ask you where you've been," she said, relieved that she didn't sound as rattled by him as she felt. "Working at the station, right?"

He held up his hands in a gesture of surrender. "Guilty!" he said with a laugh. "Actually, that's what I wanted to talk to you about, Elizabeth," he went on, suddenly serious. "I think I've stumbled onto something really major, and I want you to work with me on it."

The tone of his voice made her stop and face him. "What is it?"

Elizabeth listened quietly but intently while Tom told her about looking through the files of the athletics office for some background material on the basketball team, finding the letter about the loan, and becoming curious about Marotta's grades. Her eyes widened as he explained the theory he was forming that the jocks got special perks and privileges.

All the while two thoughts were going through her mind: *This guy is really sharp* and *Todd*.

"So, what do you say?" Tom asked when he'd finished.

Elizabeth shook her head. "I'd say that the police force lost a terrific detective when you decided to be an investigative reporter."

Tom didn't take compliments well, but for a second he looked really pleased. "What about you, though?" he pressed. "I can't do the groundwork myself because of my reputation here. I need somebody really good who I can trust completely. Will you work with me on this?"

As hurt as she was by what had happened between her and Todd, Elizabeth knew in her heart that though Todd might have some special privileges as a varsity athlete, he would never take any kind of bribe. And she also knew that Todd understood how much journalism meant to her. He would want her to do what she'd always done: tell the truth.

Tom touched her arm. "Look, Elizabeth, I know you and Todd Wilkins—"

"Of course I'll work with you," Elizabeth said, cutting him off. "If your hunch is right, then it's our duty to prove it."

She almost thought he was going to take her into his arms, he looked so happy. But he didn't take her into his arms. He shook her hand.

"Hey, blondie! Want a ride?"

Jessica stopped right in the middle of something she was saying to Isabella and Denise Waters as though someone had pulled out her plug.

Mike! her heart screamed. *It's Mike! He's right there beside you! It's him!*

Trying not to show the ecstasy she was feeling, Jessica turned to the blood-red Corvette and the dark, handsome man sitting inside it. The passenger door opened as if by magic.

"What were you saying, Jess?" Denise asked.

But Jessica was already in the Corvette—and in Michael McAllery's arms.

"I think your friends are trying to get your attention," Mike whispered when they finally broke for air.

"Um . . ." Jessica murmured, her mouth against his neck. This close to Mike, the only thing she could think of was him—holding him, kissing

43

him, inhaling his scent, melting under his touch. Isabella and Denise could be doing headstands for all Jessica cared—she wasn't going to miss one second of this.

Someone was knocking on the window. "Jessica!" Isabella called. "Do you want to meet us at the café or what?"

Mike slipped a hand under her jacket and around her waist. "You going somewhere with the girls?" he asked, his voice as soft as the line of kisses he was tracing up and down her face.

"Um . . ."

"Jessica! Do you want us to meet you at the café? Denise has to go back to her room and change anyway. We could meet you in about an hour."

"Because if you want to go with your friends, I won't try to stop you, baby. I don't want to ruin your plans."

"Jessica!"

"You're not ruining anything," Jessica managed to say despite the shivers running through her body. "I don't have any plans."

"Because if you're not going with your friends, maybe we could go someplace a little more comfortable."

"We're leaving, Jess." It was Denise's voice. "We'll see you later. Nice talking to you, Mike."

"That sounds great," Jessica answered, her voice low.

His hands moved across her body. "Don't you

want to say good-bye to your friends?"

"What friends?" Jessica asked as he leaned down to kiss her again.

Celine was sitting in a dark corner of the campus coffeehouse, watching William White the way a cat watches a bird.

Look at him, she said to herself. *Rich, conceited, attractive as sin* . . . Her eyes moved from the handsome, unsmiling face to the lean, muscular body slouched against the booth he was sitting in alone. But it wasn't really his wealth or his looks that attracted Celine, and she knew it. It was *him.* William White was the person Celine Boudreaux wanted to be. She wanted to have that effortless arrogance, that casual contempt for everybody else. She didn't want to have to constantly prove to herself that she was beautiful and desirable; she wanted to know it the way William White knew it, with every cell he possessed.

Celine's eyes narrowed. *Can it really be true?* she wondered. *Can someone like William have a crush on the Little Princess?*

Celine sipped her espresso. She'd observed William watching Elizabeth Wakefield now and then, but she hadn't really taken it seriously. If Celine couldn't tempt him with her lush, sensuous looks and wild nature, what could he possibly see in Little Miss America with her boring prettiness and golden-girl perfection? If Celine was a challenge,

45

Elizabeth was a tranquilizer.

She scraped her long, gold-colored nails along the table. No, she hadn't taken William's interest in Elizabeth seriously until this morning. But this morning when she woke up, there was a single miniature white rose in a soda bottle on Elizabeth's desk. It had taken Celine a few minutes to remember why the sight of the flower, brilliant in the sunlight, disturbed her so much.

And then it had come back to her. Last night at the party she'd been holding a rose when she tried to talk to William, and he'd taken it away from her. There must, of course, be more than one small white rose in Southern California, but there wasn't a doubt in Celine's mind that the one on Elizabeth's desk was the one William had been holding when he disappeared last night. He'd iced her completely, and then gone out to find Princess Pill. Celine's nails dug into the worn wood. Someone was going to pay for that. Two someones.

She could take care of that stupid Elizabeth easily enough. It was so much fun to spread stories and rumors about her. William was trickier. She couldn't tell him many lies about Elizabeth because he knew Celine too well; he wouldn't believe her. She was going to have to get at him some other way.

Pushing her empty cup across the table, Celine got to her feet. She picked up the shopping bags on the floor beside her chair, and slow and graceful as a cat moving in for the pounce, crossed the coffee-house.

"Why, William," she purred, sliding into the booth beside him so quickly that he couldn't stop her. "Imagine running into you again so soon. Where did you get to last night? I turned away for one minute and you were gone."

"Did somebody ask you to sit down here, Celine, or have you started hearing voices?"

Celine rested her chin on her hands. "I wouldn't be too rude to me if I were you, William White. Because it just so happens that I know something that you don't know. Something you might like to know." She touched his wrist. "Something you might like to know very much."

He raised his eyebrows, his mouth a smirk. "Oh, really? And what's that?"

Celine smiled, as a cat smiles after it's caught its prey. "The name of my roommate," she said.

Chapter Three

"I hope you don't mind me dropping in like this," Alison Quinn said. "But Isabella said you were here."

"Oh, of course not," Jessica said. She smiled her brightest and most enthusiastic smile.

It was a lucky thing she was ready for this. She had been lying in her bed, the covers over her head, remembering every detail of last night with Mike. Dreaming of what their next date would be like. Waiting for his call. But then she'd heard Isabella leave, and she'd decided that even a girl who was madly in love could use a cup of coffee. And that was when she found Isabella's note: *Alison Q. phoned. She needs to talk to you. Will be over soon. Love, Isabella.* Jessica had just enough time to get washed and dressed before Alison was knocking on the door.

Alison sat down on the couch without waiting

to be asked. "I guess you're wondering why I had to see you so urgently."

"Well, yes . . . I am . . ." Jessica lied. She'd actually been too busy thinking about Michael McAllery to give Alison Quinn much thought at all. The smile vanished from her face as something truly awful occurred to her.

Alison smiled regally, reading her thoughts. "Don't worry, Jessica, it isn't about you and the Thetas. Not specifically, anyway."

"Thank goodness." A sigh of relief escaped Jessica as she sat in the chair across from Alison. "You had me worried for a second."

Alison's smile became a little less comforting. "It does *concern* you, though, I'm afraid," she said, smoothing out a tiny wrinkle in her skirt.

Jessica looked into Alison's chilly gray eyes. For the first time in nearly twenty-four hours every thought of Mike went out of her head. "Liz!" she blurted. "It's Elizabeth, isn't it?"

This time the smile was approving. "Got it in one." Alison leaned back, her expression suddenly serious. "Let's not play games, okay, Jessica? You know and I know that the Thetas are practically obligated to pledge you and your sister because of your mother. Not that we don't want to pledge *you*, of course. *You* we love. But Elizabeth . . ." Alison shrugged, as though the problems with Elizabeth were so many and so awful that she didn't know where to begin.

"Elizabeth's been going through a difficult time," Jessica said quickly, her brain rushing ahead, creating traumas for her twin. "She—"

"Just isn't Theta material," Alison filled in. "You are. You are exactly what we look for. But Elizabeth . . ." Again she trailed off, defeated by the enormity of Elizabeth Wakefield's shortcomings. "We were very unhappy about the incident with Peter Wilbourne. You could be forgiven. You didn't know how much Peter dislikes Danny. And no one's saying that Peter wasn't out of line, attacking Danny like that, because he was. But Elizabeth made a spectacle of herself." Alison crossed her legs, flicking an invisible piece of lint from her sleeve. "Still, we were willing to overlook it. After her behavior yesterday, though—walking out in the middle of the tea like that—I'm not sure we can overlook it anymore."

"You mean you're not going to pledge her?" Jessica had warned her twin that this might happen, but still it came as a shock. More and more she seemed to be leaving her sister behind. The sensation made her feel unexpectedly lonely and vulnerable.

Alison made a sour little face. "We can't *not* pledge her," she said crisply. "Not unless we don't pledge you. I mean, I suppose she could turn us down . . ." Alison smiled as though this idea was so ridiculous she was almost embarrassed to mention it. "But there is no way we can pledge you and not pledge Elizabeth. You're seen as a package deal."

50

"But that's not fair!"

"Life's not fair." Alison shook her head. "That's why I'm here, Jessica. Magda and I have discussed it thoroughly, and if we're going to pledge your sister, she's going to have to assure us of her loyalty."

Jessica's stomach clenched. Elizabeth had no loyalty to the Thetas, and it wasn't going to be easy to get her to pretend she did. There were times when Elizabeth was too honest for Jessica's good. "How?" she asked bleakly.

Alison got to her feet. "We haven't quite worked that one out yet, but I'll let you know as soon as we do. In the meantime, though, I thought maybe you could have a word with Elizabeth. Tell her what I've told you. Get her to shape up a little."

"Sure," Jessica said, with an optimism she didn't feel. If Elizabeth wasn't careful, she could wind up a fat failure, but it was going to take more than Jessica to convince her of that. "I'll speak to her. As I said, she's been having a hard time. Her boyfriend—"

"I'm glad we had this talk." Alison held out her hand. "I know I speak for all the Thetas when I say that we'd really hate to lose you."

Jessica shook Alison's thin white hand. *I'd really hate for you to lose me too,* she thought.

Elizabeth marched into the television room, wondering if there was anything in the snack machines that wasn't fattening. She'd spent the afternoon going over the material Tom had given her that morning, making notes and working out the way she thought the story should be handled.

She'd gotten so involved that she'd actually forgotten to go to dinner. If she didn't want to starve to death or trek all the way across campus to the snack bar, she was going to have to find something to eat here.

Elizabeth looked at the machines with a sinking heart and a growling stomach. Cookies, chocolate, tortilla chips . . . There was nothing that wasn't guaranteed to make your thighs swell. Why hadn't anyone ever thought of selling carrot sticks and cottage cheese in vending machines?

"How am I supposed to stay on my diet when I'm surrounded by candy bars and potato chips?" Elizabeth asked aloud. "It just isn't fair."

"You can say that again."

Elizabeth flushed. She'd thought she was alone.

"If you ask me, it should be illegal to have those things in a female dorm. Everybody knows that at any given time three out of every six women are on a diet."

Elizabeth turned around. The pretty face of Nina Harper was looking at her from over the back of the couch. Only, for the first time Elizabeth could remember since she'd met Nina, her face wasn't serious, it was grinning.

Elizabeth laughed. "Don't tell me you're on a diet too! You don't need to lose weight."

"Neither do you," Nina said. She smiled wryly. "I'm sort of on the lifer's diet. You know," she said, seeing Elizabeth's puzzled look. "If I weren't on a diet, I would have to lose weight. All you have to do is put me near a pepperoni pizza and I'm a lost woman."

"Potato chips," Elizabeth said, giving the snack machine a kick. "I've been resisting those cheddar-cheese potato chips since yesterday, but now I'm so hungry I may have to succumb. I've been working all afternoon."

Nina studied her for a minute. "I'm always seeing you in the library. You work almost as hard as I do. Do you have parents with enormous expectations too?"

Elizabeth shook her head. "No, I just don't have much else to do." She smiled ruefully. "*And* I have a roommate who drives me out of my mind."

"Celine, right?"

"The one and only." Elizabeth glanced toward the ceiling. "Thank God."

Normally she wouldn't complain about someone behind her back, but Celine was the exception to every rule. And things between them were just getting worse. Yesterday morning Elizabeth had found the rose William White had given her in her wastebasket, its petals not just plucked, but crushed.

"Roommates can be difficult," Nina said mildly. "Mine's okay, but we don't really have much in common. It's bad enough that she doesn't like my

53

music, but she even complains that my hair makes too much noise."

"You must be kidding," Elizabeth said, trying not to choke with laughter. Nina's hair was in dozens of thin braids, each one held by a wooden bead at the end. "I love your hair. I think it looks great."

"Yeah, well, my roommate says it wakes her up in the night. And she goes nuts if I just shake my head when she's trying to study. That's why I go to the library so much. I can't study with her sighing and moaning all the time. And I guess the truth is, I'm a workaholic. It runs in my family." She shrugged. "What about you? Why do you want to lose weight?"

"Because I've gained some weight since school started," Elizabeth answered immediately, surprising herself. She hadn't even discussed her weight gain with Jessica, and here she was telling a stranger. "I used to be a perfect size six."

Nina stood up. "I haven't been a size six since I was ten." Nina was tall and big boned, but solidly built. "You're not going to get anything decent to eat from that machine," she said as she came over to Elizabeth. "I'm supposed to be studying for a psych test, but I could use a break. Why don't we go over to the coffeehouse? They make a great vegetable salad. If we split one, we could have enough spare calories to have some bread with it."

Elizabeth was tempted to say no. She really should go back to work. She really didn't feel like trudging across campus in the rain. She really shouldn't eat anything. A little starvation would do her good. She looked at Nina Harper's smiling face. It was one of the friendliest faces she'd encountered all semester.

Elizabeth smiled back. "Only if you promise not to let your hair make too much noise."

"You must have come home pretty late last night."

Jessica looked up from the history reading she was trying to do to kill time while she waited for Mike to call. Isabella was leaning against the wall, watching her with an expression that reminded Jessica of her mother. Jessica bit her lip. The last thing she needed right now was a lecture.

"Since when are you my mother?" she asked, laughing to keep her tone light.

"Since you've started making a public spectacle of yourself with Mike McAllery," Isabella replied, not sounding light at all. "What were you thinking yesterday? Leaving me and Denise standing there like a couple of idiots." She strode into the room, sitting at the table across from Jessica. "What time did you get in, anyway? You didn't spend the night with Mike, did you?"

Jessica couldn't hide her surprise. "Is this Isabella Ricci, the wild woman of SVU, talking?"

"No, this is Isabella Ricci, your best friend at SVU, talking." She grabbed Jessica's hand. "Listen to me, Jess, you have got to get a grip. How many times do I have to tell you? Mike is not just some college kid with a crazy streak. He's dangerous. This guy should come with a government health warning tattooed across his forehead: *This man could seriously damage your heart.*" She gave Jessica a sarcastic look. "Not to mention the damage he could do to your reputation."

"My reputation?" Furious, Jessica pushed back her chair and jumped to her feet. As good a friend as Isabella had become since school started, Jessica sometimes wished that Lila Fowler, her best friend from high school, had come to college as planned, instead of staying in Europe and marrying an Italian count. Lila wouldn't have been critical. Lila would have been supportive.

"You don't seem to understand something, Isabella," Jessica said calmly. "I'm in love with Mike. He's the man of my dreams."

"You may think he's the man of your dreams now," Isabella said ominously. "But if you're not careful, he's going to turn into the man of your nightmares."

Jessica glared back at her. "I don't have to listen to this!"

"Yes, you do!" Isabella got to her feet too. "Jessica, will you please stop thinking with your hormones? It's not just that Mike drinks and fools around with lots of different women. No one has any idea what he does for money. He might be a drug dealer, for all you know."

"You said he was a photographer," Jessica said, feeling cornered. Somehow, she'd never gotten around to actually asking Mike what he did for a living. He wasn't the kind of man who encouraged personal questions.

"I said he *used* to be a photographer. But that was a long time ago."

Jessica's cheeks were burning. "What about his father? You told me he inherited a lot of money."

"Look at the car the man drives!" Isabella shouted. "The way that guy lives, he could have gone through at least three inheritances by now."

"I don't care!" Jessica screamed. "I don't care about any of that!"

"Well, you should care. You should—"

The ringing of the telephone drowned out Isabella's words. *Saved by the bell*, thought Jessica, making a dive for the phone.

"I've been thinking about you, baby," the voice said, as smooth and supple as a snake. "I was afraid I missed you. I was afraid you might have gone out with your friends."

I may never go out with my friends again. "No, I'm right here." She lowered her voice. "I was hoping you'd call."

"I'm coming by to get you. Wait downstairs."

Jessica hung up the phone, her anger of a few minutes before replaced by joy. *I'm coming by to get you. Wait downstairs.* Without another word to

Isabella, she picked up her jacket and ran out the door.

There she was! *Be still, my catapulting heart,* he told himself. *Don't make so much noise, she'll hear you!*

Half hidden by a large potted palm, Winston Egbert gazed across the snack bar to where a beautiful young woman sat by herself, reading a novel while she ate a plate of onion rings. Winston couldn't help sighing. Watching Denise Waters eat onion rings was like watching poetry in motion.

He held his breath, trying to figure out his next move. It hadn't been easy following her here. He'd had to hang around in the lobby of Oakley Hall for hours, pretending to be waiting for someone, till she finally came out. Then he'd had to trail her from the dorm. He'd never known anyone with so many friends. They barely managed to walk a couple of yards before Denise would run into someone else she knew and stop to talk. And the whole time, of course, he'd had to keep his eye out for the blue jackets of the Sigmas.

Winston's eyes scanned the room again. Not only had he made it across campus without seeing one Sigma brother, but, miraculously, there weren't any in the snack bar, either.

This is it, Win, he told himself. *This is your chance. Go over and ask her if you can sit down. She'll say yes. She likes you. She always laughs at your jokes.*

Denise took another onion ring from her plate,

dipped it in ketchup, and lifted it to her lips. Winston thought his heart might break. It was like watching a Shakespearean sonnet eat, only better. No sonnet in the world looked or sounded or smelled like Denise Waters.

Go, Winston urged himself. *Go now. Good grief, you're her buddy. She borrows your hair dryer. She lends you tapes. She shared her popcorn with you when you watched the television movie Wednesday night. She even told you when it was all right to look. This woman isn't a stranger, Win, she's a friend.*

Winston took a deep breath and stepped from behind the palm. Nothing happened. Because a large, meaty hand had suddenly locked itself onto his shoulder.

"Win, old pal!" Bill was shouting. "Win, we've been looking all over for you. Where've you been?"

Winston laughed nervously. "Oh, around. Just around." It wasn't easy, but he forced himself to smile.

Bill's arm slid around his shoulders. "Let's go get a burger, pal," he said as he propelled Winston toward the line. "My treat."

"Your treat?"

Two other Sigmas followed, making their usual racket. Winston glanced over at Denise. There was no way he could approach her now. After seeing Winston with these guys, Denise would forget what a nice, normal human being he was. She'd think he was one of them.

"You know, this is a very fortuitous meeting," Bill was saying as he picked up a tray. "Really fortuitous, Winston. Because I've been meaning to ask you for a little favor, and the object of that little favor happens to be right over there."

A chill, dank suspicion engulfed Winston's heart. It couldn't be. It just couldn't be. Bill couldn't be interested in Denise. Winston hadn't done anything to deserve it. Surely the gods wouldn't be this unkind to him. Winston stared into Bill's big-man smile. It was a good thing he'd been so preoccupied with waiting for Denise today that he'd forgotten to eat lunch, or he'd probably throw up about now.

"Oh, really?" he croaked. "What's that, Bill?"

Bill leaned so close, Winston could smell the grape bubble gum he was chewing. "I was wondering if you could introduce me to Denise Waters. I mean, I know her by sight and everything, but she's always been really standoffish to me. I thought that maybe you and I could go over there and sit with her. You know, once she got to see what a good guy I am, she might warm up."

Winston could only stare at Bill in horror. A girl like Denise might incinerate a guy like Bill, but she wasn't going to warm up to him. And she wasn't going to warm up to anybody who tried to set them up, either. Even if Winston could impersonate Donald Duck singing the telephone jingle, she would never go out with him after that.

"She's a friend of yours, right?" Bill asked. He

winked. "She's in your dorm, right? You two wash your faces together. You've seen her with goop in her hair. Be a real pal, Win. Just give me an intro."

For weeks Winston had been thinking of Denise. He even dreamed about her. She was intelligent, she was beautiful, she was nice. They made each other laugh. She was everything he'd ever wanted in a woman. For weeks he'd been working up enough courage to ask her out, and here he'd finally gotten himself to the brink—and what happened? Bill happened.

Winston's fantasies were disintegrating in front of his eyes. He looked over at Denise. She was leaving! Her guardian angel must have whispered in her ear that Bill was on his way over to put the moves on her. She was definitely on her way out.

"Oh, gee, will you look at that!" Winston said, his voice filled with disappointment. "She's going, Bill. We're too late."

Bill watched Denise disappear through the door. "Well, you can forget about that hamburger then, Win."

"What did she ever see in him?" William asked. "He looks like he should be dating Barbie."

Celine followed William's gaze across the jammed living room of the Zeta house to where Todd Wilkins and his basketball buddies were demonstrating a play for a circle of admiring girls. *You mean, what did he ever see in a wet towel like*

Elizabeth, Celine thought. She shrugged. "I really don't know, William." She gave him a meaningful look. "It's a mystery to me what attracts certain people to certain other people."

He wasn't paying attention. "You're sure they've broken up?"

"Sure as the Mississippi is wide," Celine said. She pointed to the attractive redhead at Todd's side. "That's his new girlfriend, Lauren Hill. I hear they're very close." She lit a cigarette, blowing a thin stream of smoke past William's handsome face.

William choked. "I wish you'd give those things up, Celine," he snapped. "Next to your personality they're one of the most unappealing things about you."

"Why, William White," Celine drawled, floating a perfect ring of smoke in front of him. "Are you trying to turn my head with flattery?"

"I'm going to go get another drink before you asphyxiate me. I'll be back."

Celine watched him cross the room. Aloof and apart, he stood out in the crowd of normal, average students like a diamond in a bag of peanuts. Celine blew another smoke ring into the air. For all his aloofness, people were drawn to him. She watched them stop him as he moved toward the refreshment table. Celine moistened her lips with the tip of her tongue. She knew he'd be back. It didn't matter how much he insulted her; the important thing was that he was no longer pretending she didn't exist. Now that William knew she lived with Elizabeth, he needed her. They were allies. Partners. Celine smiled to herself. William, of course, thought that he was using *her*.

She knew it was the other way around.

Jessica sat behind Mike on the customized lowrider as they sped through the night, the lights of the buildings flashing past them like stars. She felt as though she were flying.

If my parents could see me now, they would have a fit. The Wakefields hated motorcycles because of the accident Elizabeth had had her junior year, and they'd forbidden the twins ever to ride on them again. But Ned and Alice Wakefield couldn't see Jessica now. They stopped at a light and Jessica put her lips to the cracked leather of Mike's jacket, trying to commit the smell and feel of it to memory. It didn't really matter if her parents could see her. She wasn't a child anymore, after all. She was a woman. If she wanted to ride behind Mike on his motorcycle, there was no way in the world anyone could prevent her.

At last the bike pulled to a stop in a parking lot and she jumped off. "That was fantastic!" she cried. "Absolutely fantastic! That's the most incredible machine I've ever seen." She laughed, throwing herself into his arms. "I didn't even know you owned a motorcycle."

He smiled. "There's a lot you don't know about me."

Jessica rested her head against his chest with a happy sigh. And then her eyes fell on the building in front of them. She'd thought he was taking her out for a late-night snack, but she'd been wrong. It was an apartment building: a large, white apartment building with a green door and cacti out front. A building Jessica had seen many times before.

"What's this?" she asked, trying to hide her surprise.

"I thought it was about time you saw where I live." Mike put his arm around her and started leading her up the flagstone path.

"You could have told me this was where we were coming," she said, sounding a little more petulant than she'd intended. This was the building where her brother, Steven, and his girlfriend, Billie lived. It wasn't a happy coincidence.

"Well, now you know." He gave her a squeeze. "I'm tired of making out with you in the car, Jess. It wrinkles my clothes and it cramps my style." He opened the front door. "And besides, I'm not a teenager, even if you are."

Jessica followed him up to his apartment, the exhilaration of the ride forgotten. She hated it when he teased her about her age. Just because she was young didn't mean she wasn't grown up. She was a woman.

"Well, this is it," Mike said. He unlocked the door and ushered her inside. "My humble home."

"My God!" Jessica tried to be extra cool when she was around Mike, but this time she couldn't hide her shock. "This place is unbelievable. I've never seen anything like it in my life!"

Mike's apartment was the exact size and layout of Steven's, but all similarities ended there. Steven's was just a run-of-the-mill student apartment, furnished with bits and pieces people had given him or he'd found in secondhand stores. But Mike's was a state-of-the-art bachelor apartment, so expensively and perfectly decorated it looked like a movie set. It didn't look like a place where a real person lived. Jessica looked over at Mike. And Mike wasn't a real person. He'd stepped right out of a dream.

"So you think it's okay?"

"*Okay?* Yes, I think it's okay."

Jessica stood at the entrance to the living room for a few minutes, just looking at the highly polished wood floors scattered with afghan carpets; the oversize sofa and armchairs, upholstered in silk, the slatted wooden blinds in the windows; and the large, old-fashioned green fan that looked like a propeller hanging from the ceiling. One wall was lined with shelves filled with books, and another was taken up by a large-screen television, a VCR, and a black-and-chrome music center. The lighting was subtle and indirect.

Isabella's voice started yammering in her ear. *How does he get his money, Jess? What does he do? A*

'64 Corvette . . . a custom-made motorcycle . . . this apartment . . . He must do something, Jess. He didn't win it all in a game show.

Mike's arms encircled her, causing Isabella's voice to vanish back into the air. "I'm glad you like it," he whispered. "I want you to feel at home here, baby. I want you to feel relaxed."

Jessica leaned into him. If she felt any more relaxed, her bones would dissolve. "I do feel at home," she whispered back. "I love—I love it here."

He kissed her ear. "Then why don't we lie down on the couch, put a video in the machine, and not watch it for a couple of hours?"

She didn't have to answer. He'd already lifted her in his arms and was carrying her across the room.

Later, when a second video was playing unnoticed and they were lying on the couch in each other's arms, exchanging small, personal details about themselves, Jessica remembered Isabella's questions. Mike's breath was as warm as sunlight on her face. His body was so close, she could hardly tell where hers ended and his began. The mood between them was so close and so intimate that she felt she could ask him now.

She ran her fingers through his long, soft hair. "What is it you said you do for a living?" she asked in a near whisper, straining to make her voice casual and easy.

Mike flicked off the movie, tossing the remote

across the floor. He moved so that he was over her, his mouth a kiss away, his eyes staring into her heart.

"I didn't say."

Sometimes, when Celine was in a really good mood and was feeling wanted and at peace with the world, she would come into the dorm quietly late at night. She would unlock the door to her room softly. Instead of turning on the overhead light, or even the lamp on her desk, she would undress by the tiny night-light Elizabeth had put in the outlet by the door. She wouldn't throw her shoes across the room. She wouldn't bang into things. She wouldn't turn on the radio or light up a cigarette.

Tonight, however, Celine was not in a good mood. It had been a terrific party, full of laughter and music—the sort of party that made you feel as though you had a million friends and would always be beautiful and young.

But in the end, William had spoiled it for her. She'd been charming and funny and full of conversation, yet the longer the evening wore on, the more sullen and silent he'd become. Celine was certain that if she could get close enough to him, she could make William White fall in love with her. That was her plan. To make him fall in love with her and then to break his heart into more pieces than there were grains of sand on the

California shore. But to make him forget Elizabeth and fall for her was going to be harder than she'd thought.

"You're thinking about *her*, aren't you?" Celine had finally asked, only just managing to keep the jealousy and revulsion out of her voice. "You haven't stopped thinking about her all night."

He'd turned to her, his skin so white, his mouth so soft, his eyes so hard. "And who else would I be thinking of?"

Remembering that moment and the way William had looked at her, as though she were some form of pond life and not a beautiful young woman herself, Celine marched down the corridor of Dickenson Hall, a lighted cigarette in her hand, and threw open the door to her room with a bang. She snapped on the desk lamp and hurled herself onto her bed.

The effect was instantaneous. A blond head rose up from the opposite bed, squinting and rubbing the sleep from her eyes.

"Celine?" The blue-green eyes slowly opened. "What do you think you're doing?"

But Celine wasn't going to listen to one of Elizabeth's lectures tonight. Tonight wasn't a night for arguing. Tonight was a night for claws and blood.

"You missed a great party, Lizzie," she said sweetly. "A really great party. One of your favorite people was there."

Elizabeth was sitting up, anger replacing sleepiness. "Celine, are you out of your mind? What do you—"

"Todd," Celine said. "Todd was there. With that lovely girl, what's her name? Lauren? Lauren Hill?"

Elizabeth was staring at her now, her expression a mixture of hurt and disbelief.

Celine's smile grew. "They certainly have gotten very close very fast, haven't they? But then, she is so very, very lovely." Celine's eyes flashed. "Slender . . . pretty . . . vivacious . . ." Celine blew a cloud of smoke across the room.

"By the way," she said, feeling much better all of a sudden. "Todd was asking about you. 'How's Liz?' he asked."

Celine's smile grew even bigger and brighter. "You don't have to worry, Lizzie," she purred. "I didn't tell him you were still sulky and putting on weight. I told him you were fine."

Chapter
Four

Even as Jessica gradually gained consciousness, she wondered where she was. She could tell from the sounds outside and the feel of the air that she wasn't where she was supposed to be. When she opened her eyes she wasn't going to see the deep-raspberry walls of the room she shared with Isabella, or Isabella herself in the opposite bed, lying flat on her back on her paisley sheets. The question was, What was she going to see?

Slowly Jessica opened her eyes. The room was dark, only a few determined shafts of light managing to struggle through the blinds. She looked around. Books . . . television . . . fan . . . Mike's apartment! She was still at Mike's. She was on the couch, still wearing the clothes she'd been wearing the night before, though now they were rumpled and her blouse was unbuttoned. And there, his head resting between her arm and her breast, was Mike, still wearing his jeans and a T-shirt. His dark hair fanned over her skin, his sensuous lips parted in a smile.

Jessica had no memory of falling asleep. She remembered snuggling against him, intoxicated by his smell. She remembered the room melting away as she lost herself to his hands and his lips. But she didn't remember closing her eyes. They must both have passed out, exhausted from so many passionate kisses. She leaned over and rested her cheek on the top of his head.

I can't believe it! she thought as she stared down at him, almost hypnotized, just watching him sleep. *I can't believe I spent the whole night with a guy!*

What more proof did she need that she really was a sophisticated woman of the world? There was nothing she couldn't do now. Wait till she told Lila! Wait till she told Lila what a wonderful, incredible night she'd had.

A frown appeared on Jessica's face. Lila wasn't here anymore. Lila was in Italy, married to a count. Isabella was here. And Isabella wasn't going to think it was wonderful or incredible at all. Isabella was going to think it was shocking. She was going to be full of more warnings and lectures and tales of gloom. Jessica sighed. She would have to tell Isabella something else. That she'd stayed with Steven, or even with Elizabeth.

She would save the truth for a letter to Lila. The frown deepened. Lila wasn't going to think Jessica's night was so wonderful and incredible either. What was so wonderful about sleeping on a couch in your jeans and a flannel shirt? Lila was a married woman.

"Morning, baby."

Jessica looked over. That smile was more dazzling than any sunny morning. "Morning, yourself."

He nuzzled against her, his mouth in her hair. "You sure are a nice thing to wake up to," he said, his voice still fuzzy with sleep. "But I guess all the guys tell you that."

She gave him a shove. "What are you talking about? I never woke—"

Mike laughed, lifting himself up on one arm to look at her. "Chill out, Jess. I know you're still a little girl. You made that pretty clear last night."

She hadn't thought it was possible to get mad at him, but she was almost mad now. What was it with men? If you weren't a virgin, they wondered if you slept around, and if you were a virgin, they accused you of being a little girl.

"Hey!" Seeing the expression on her face, he leaned over and kissed her on the tip of her nose. "I'm just teasing you, baby. Don't get yourself all wound up."

Jessica smiled back, but she couldn't help wondering if Lila's husband called her "baby."

Mike got up and stretched. "How about some coffee? I could use a whole pot of it poured over my head. I feel like I slept in a box."

Jessica laughed. "I'd love a—" She shook her

wrist. Could it really be eight thirty? "Oh, my God! I've got a philosophy seminar in forty-five minutes that I can't miss. I've got to go!"

Mike turned in the doorway. "Why don't you blow off your classes today? Hang out with me. We can take the bike up the coast. I know a beautiful little beach. . . ."

Jessica was already on her feet, pulling on her shoes. "I can't, Mike, I really can't. I'm not doing so well in my classes right now. I can't afford to cut this seminar. It's going to figure a lot in our final grade." She didn't need to mention that she wasn't doing so well in her classes because she spent all her free time thinking about him.

"Suit yourself. There's a brand-new toothbrush in the medicine cabinet. It's yours if you want it."

"I don't have time." It was bad enough that she was going to have Isabella on her case for spending the night with Mike; she didn't need to miss class, too. She snatched up her bag and her jacket. "I'll just have to have gorilla breath for one morning."

Jessica opened the door, but before she could rush through it, two strong arms wrapped themselves around her.

"Hey," Mike whispered. "What sort of a guy do you think I am? I don't want people saying my baby's a gorilla. Go brush your teeth and then I'll run you to school."

My life has fallen into a routine, Steven Wakefield

73

was thinking as he threw the garbage into the black plastic can in front of his building. Monday mornings he emptied the trash. Tuesday evenings Billie had a class and he picked up pizza on his way home. On Wednesdays, Billie cooked and he did the laundry. Thursdays he had late classes and she picked up something for supper. Fridays he cooked and they usually rented a video and stayed in.

Steven looked up at the cloudless, blue morning sky. *But it's a nice routine,* he told himself. Peaceful. Secure. There were no major problems to be overcome, no major traumas to adjust to. He had Billie, he had school, everything was going well for him.

I'm a lucky guy, Steven was thinking as he turned back to the front door.

The smile shriveled on his lips. Standing there on the stoop, for everyone to see, was Mike Mr. Attitude McAllery, locked in a passionate kiss with his very own sister.

Steven clenched his fists as his blood began to churn. He was used to seeing Mike McAllery with women. Mike McAllery had more women coming in and out than the local beauty parlor. Steven was also was used to seeing Mike kissing his women in public. But he wasn't used to seeing him kissing his little sister. Not at eight thirty in the morning!

"What the hell is going on here?"

The couple on the stoop didn't look over. They were too involved in mashing their mouths together to even have heard Steven's roar.

"Hey! McAllery! I'm talking to you, you low-life. What the hell do you think you're doing?"

Very slowly, like an elephant who thinks an ant may have just walked over its foot, Mike McAllery pulled back, his arms still around Jessica, and turned to Steven. Jessica had the decency to look horrified and embarrassed. But Mike didn't even blink.

"I live here," Mike said. "That's what I'm doing. I'm living here. What are you doing?"

"I'll tell you!" Steven shouted, already up the path and grabbing hold of Jessica to pull her away. "I'm going to hit you so hard in the mouth it'll be a year before you kiss anyone again!"

"Steven!" Jessica shrieked. She pushed him away. "What are you doing? Have you lost your mind?"

"Me? Have I lost *my* mind? Jessica, what are you doing with this creep? What are you doing at eight thirty in the morning kissing this creep?" He reached for her again.

Mike McAllery stepped in front of Jessica, laying one hand flat on Steven's chest. "Before I make this guy part of the fertilizer, Jess," he said in his slow, calm way, "you want to tell me who he is?"

Steven knocked his hand away. "I'll tell you who I am, you piece of garbage. I'm her brother."

McAllery smiled. "Is that true?" He looked over his shoulder at Jessica. "Is this vigilante really your brother?"

Jessica nodded. Steven noticed that though she

was looking at him, she was holding on to Mike.

Mike turned back to Steven. "Well, let me tell you who *I* am, Superbrother. I'm Jessica's boyfriend. And that gives me top billing, as I see it." He stretched out his arm and Jessica stepped into it. "Come on, baby," he said, giving Steven an arrogant smile. "Let's get going before big brother here makes you late for school."

Steven felt as though his blood had been freeze-dried. Not long ago, Elizabeth had turned up on his doorstep in tears in the middle of the night. Elizabeth had always been popular and sure of herself in high school, but college had thrown her, and she was miserable with loneliness and insecurity. Billie thought that all Elizabeth needed was some time to find her feet, but Steven couldn't stop worrying about her. And now this. Now Jessica had turned up on his doorstep in the middle of a passionate kiss with a creep. What was it with his sisters? Were they trying to drive him nuts?

Steven was still standing in front of the building, staring down the street in the direction the motorcycle had gone, when Billie came looking for him.

"Steven! What are you doing out here, gazing into space? I was getting worried."

He turned to her. Her pretty face was drawn with concern. "You should be worried," he said, shaking his head. "My sister Jessica just left here with Mike McAllery."

"What?"

"You heard me. Jessica is seeing that ape Mc-Allery. She was here. With him. Kissing. They just left."

The concern on Billie's face disappeared. "I think you're overreacting a little, Steven. Mike McAllery may be a character, but he is not an ape."

Steven stared at her as though he'd never seen her before. "What? Are you saying that you approve? Are you saying that you think it's just fine for my sister to hang around with a womanizing cretin like that?"

She was smiling. Billie was actually smiling.

"Oh, come on, Steven." Billie took his hand. "I'm not saying it's fine; I'm just saying it's not really any of your business. Jessica's a woman now."

He pulled his hand away. "And what's that supposed to mean?"

Billie gave him an exasperated look. "It's not supposed to mean anything. It just—"

"Are you suggesting that Jessica might actually be *sleeping* with that delinquent? Is that what you're suggesting?"

She looked as though she might start laughing. "College people do sleep together, you know, Steven. It has been heard of."

Steven glared at her. As much as he cared about Billie, there were times when she baffled him. He knew what she was getting at, of course. She thought that it was hypocritical of him to live with her and then be so outraged that his sister might be having a serious relationship. What she didn't seem to understand was that there was no connection between his and Billie's relationship and Jessica and Mike McAllery's. How would she like it if it were *her* sister running around with a man with a vintage Corvette and no visible means of support?

"They sleep with responsible, trustworthy people they can have a real relationship with, Billie," Steven said stiffly. "Not with bums who have more girlfriends than Ford has cars."

She touched his shoulder. "Steven," she said patiently, "don't you think that you may be exaggerating just a little? I know he gets around, but—"

"No, I don't think I'm exaggerating. McAllery is a man of the world and Jessica's still in her teens." He could hear his voice getting louder, but he couldn't stop it. "What if he hurts her, Billie? Have you thought about that? What if he winds up breaking her heart?"

"Stop shouting at me, Steven!" Billie turned back to the door and yanked it open. "It's not your heart he'll be breaking," she said, standing halfway in the building. "It's Jessica's. Why don't you let her worry about it?"

"Muesli, skim milk, one small apple, black coffee . . . Well, what do you know? You and I are having the exact same breakfast. I guess this meeting of the SVU Diet Till You Drop club can now begin."

Elizabeth, who had been staring vacantly into

her muesli, looked up to see Nina putting her tray down on the table across from her.

"You have no idea what willpower it took not to have frosted cornflakes and a doughnut this morning," Elizabeth said with a laugh. "I slept so badly last night I could use a massive dose of sugar."

Nina flopped into her chair. "You don't look so good, now that you mention it." She tilted her head, scrutinizing Elizabeth's face. "What's wrong? Dreams of pepperoni pizza and triple chocolate mousse keep you awake?"

Elizabeth sighed. "I wish."

"What's the matter, Elizabeth?" Nina's face was filled with genuine concern. "What could have happened between yesterday afternoon when we had such a good time together and this morning to make you look so miserable?"

"Celine went to a party."

"Yeah? And then what? She brought the band back with her?"

Elizabeth shook her head. "I almost wish she had. She woke me up to tell me that Todd was at the party."

Nina's eyebrows went up. "Oh. I get it." Nina poured skim milk over her muesli and dug in her spoon. In the course of a very long evening, one of the things that Nina and Elizabeth had discussed in some depth was Todd. "Let me guess. Todd wasn't alone."

"He was with Lauren."

"How nice of Celine to tell you," Nina said through a mouthful of cereal. "I don't suppose she went into any of the gory details, did she? I'm sure she'd want to spare your feelings."

Elizabeth smirked. "How did you guess? She also made sure she mentioned how slim and vivacious Lauren is." She pushed her cereal bowl away. "I may never eat again."

Nina pushed it back. "Cut it out, will you, Liz? You may have put on a few pounds, but you're still pretty slim and vivacious yourself. You've got a lot more on the ball than Lauren Hill, that's for sure." She chewed another spoonful of muesli.

"It's not that so much," Elizabeth said miserably. "It's that I really miss Todd. I'm beginning to think I was wrong to let the relationship just end like that, but it's too late."

"Maybe, maybe not." Nina gave her a thoughtful look. "I wouldn't let Celine wind me up if I were you," she said slowly. "Celine loves to cause trouble, especially for you." She pointed her spoon at Elizabeth. "Believe me, if that girl's mouth were a gun, it would be an uzi automatic."

Something in Nina's tone made Elizabeth look at her closely. "What do you mean, *especially for me*?"

Nina shrugged. "Let's just say that until I actually talked to you yesterday, it would have been easy for me to assume that the person with roommate problems was Celine, not you."

"What?"

"Look," Nina said, the beads on her braids clicking as she leaned forward. "I didn't know whether or not I should mention this, but Celine goes around telling the wildest stories about you. . . ."

Elizabeth wasn't even sure why she should feel so surprised or so betrayed. She should have known Celine would be gossiping about her behind her back. "And do people believe her?"

Nina made a face. "I think a lot of people believed her at first. You know how sweet and charming she can be. And you were so quiet and reserved. . . ." She turned her attention back to her cereal. "To be completely honest, Liz," Nina went on slowly, not meeting Elizabeth's eyes, "I believed her myself at first. Until I started seeing you in the library all the time and noticed you around campus. Then I started to suspect that Celine wasn't being too economical with the truth. I think other people are beginning to catch on too. I saw her at a party last week, and the only people who would talk to her were guys who see better than they think."

Elizabeth groaned. "Oh, great. I'll bet she's been telling Todd stories too."

"That's what I'm trying to say," Nina explained. "You don't know. Maybe it would be worth talking to Todd. Even if it is just for your own peace of mind."

Elizabeth picked up her coffee cup. "Maybe," she said. "Maybe it would."

*   *   *

Jessica saw them as soon as they came around the corner. Isabella and Denise were standing on the pavement outside the lecture hall where her seminar was being given, deep in conversation. At the sound of the bike's engine, they broke off and turned around. Then again, everyone on the sidewalk was staring at the bike as it rumbled to a stop in front of a No Parking sign.

Jessica leaned over Mike's shoulder as he turned off the ignition. "You certainly know how to make an entrance," she whispered.

Mike grinned. "It's not me, it's the killer Kawasaki engine."

She pulled off her helmet and shook out her hair. "Well, whatever it is, it sure is effective. Everybody's gaping at us."

Mike turned and slipped his arm around her. "Why don't we give them something to talk about?"

Pressed against him, his mouth on hers, it was as though the rest of the world just stopped. Nothing mattered—not Steven, not school, not her friends, not what people might think or say. She wouldn't have cared if the entire state of California were gathered on the sidewalk beside them, watching them kiss. All that mattered was that she was in Mike's arms, and that was where she wanted to stay.

The clock in the lecture-hall tower began to chime and students began to disappear.

Jessica pulled back, glancing toward the curb

again. Isabella and Denise had not disappeared. They were still standing there, staring at her with open disapproval.

Mike's eyes followed hers. "What do you say, Jess?" he asked. "You want to stay with your snobby friends? Or you want to go to the beach with me?"

"We'll have to stop by the dorm first," Jessica said. "So I can pick up my bikini."

"Strike while the iron is hot," Elizabeth mumbled to herself as she hurried across campus to the athlete's dorm where Todd lived. "Seize the moment. She who hesitates is lost."

What Elizabeth had told Nina was true. After Celine woke her up last night, taunting her about seeing Todd with Lauren, she had tossed and turned all night. Every time she drifted off to sleep, images of herself and Todd haunted her dreams. She missed him. Now that the insecurity she'd been feeling when she first got to college was beginning to fade, she could see that he'd been right all along. It was time that their relationship changed. It was time to grow up.

Nina was right. Elizabeth owed it to herself to talk to Todd. What did she really know? Just because he was seen around campus with Lauren Hill didn't mean he didn't miss Elizabeth. He might be laughing and having a good time on the outside, but inside he could be nursing a broken heart just as she was.

83

The ultramodern glass-and-steel dorm came into view. Elizabeth slowed down. "Nothing ventured, nothing gained," she told herself as she entered the building.

"You're doing the right thing," she assured herself as she got into the elevator. She knocked on Todd's door. "I'm *sure* you're doing the right thing." She knocked again.

"Liz!" He must have just gotten up. His shirt was unbuttoned, and he held a tube of toothpaste in his hand. "I—I thought you were Mark."

"I'm sorry to just show up like this," she said, her words coming out in a rush, "but I really have to talk to you."

He stared back at her as though she'd suggested they go bungee jumping. "Now?"

Elizabeth nodded. "I know this is sudden, and you probably have a class to go to—I do too—but I don't want to put this off any longer. We keep avoiding each other, like there's nothing left to discuss, but you just don't end a relationship like ours in ten minutes. . . ."

He didn't nod. He didn't speak. He just continued staring at her, his face wary and his body tense.

"Do you?" Elizabeth persisted.

Apparently he thought you did, if the expression on his face was anything to go by.

"Todd—" Elizabeth took a step forward. "Couldn't we just talk for a minute? There are a couple of things I really have to say."

He glanced over his shoulder, as though he'd heard something. "Maybe later, Liz. Why don't we meet later in the student center? My last class ends at five today. We could meet up then. Have a cup of coffee or something—"

"But I don't want to wait till five. I want to talk to you now."

Desperation was making her voice whine. Somehow, when she'd imagined this scene, she hadn't been whining and pleading. She'd been strong and clear. But when she'd imagined this scene, Todd hadn't been standing there like the Great Wall of China, stony and silent and blocking her way. He'd been welcoming her with open arms.

She'd come too far to stop now, though. She had to see it through. "Todd, please . . . I miss you so much. You were right and I was wrong. It was time our relationship changed. It was—"

"No, you were right, Liz. That side of things is over for us. We shouldn't be any more than friends. It would have been a mistake to go any further."

"Todd, I–I—"

"No, Liz, I really think—"

The bathroom door opened suddenly, sounding like the shot of a gun.

Elizabeth knew instinctively that she should turn and run, but she didn't. Instead, she looked over Todd's shoulder. Lauren Hill was standing framed in the doorway of the bathroom, wearing only Todd's practice jersey and looking sleepy and rumpled.

"Todd?" Lauren said. "Do you have the tooth-paste?"

What a dream, Tom was thinking as he and Danny left the cafeteria. Just the thought of it made him smile.

"What's with you this morning?" Danny asked, giving him a curious look. "Either there were strange chemical pollutants in my tea this morning making me see things, or you're actually happy."

Tom slung his backpack over his shoulder and gave his friend an innocent "Who, me?" look. Ever since Danny had come to terms with his own fears and stood up to Peter Wilbourne at the Halloween dance, he had been on a minicampaign for Tom to come to terms with *his* feelings as well. Tom wouldn't have stood for it from anybody else, but Danny was the nearest thing he had to a brother—now. As terrified as Tom was of being close to any-one, there was too much between him and Danny to pull away.

"Happy?" Tom repeated. "I'm not happy, Dan-iel. I'm just hyped up because of the sports scandal piece. Elizabeth is as excited as I am, and I have a hunch this one is really going to come gold."

Danny stopped at the top of the stairs. "Sure," he said. "You're hyped up. God forbid Tom Watts should ever feel happy."

Tom gave him a playful shove. "Don't you have a class to go to or something?" he asked with a laugh.

"Yeah, yeah, I'm going." Danny gave him a slap on the back. "See you later, Tombo. Only, you better stop grinning to yourself like that or everybody on this campus is going to think you're happy. Then your reputation as Mr. Ice Man will really be shot."

Tom headed toward the television studio to check on the rundown for the day. So, maybe he did feel a little happy. Last night in his dream he'd felt happier than he had in years. In two long years, to be exact, since he was a freshman.

And he'd even known he was dreaming—he'd known the whole time—but he'd still felt happy. *This is a dream*, he kept telling himself. *This is only a dream*. But it sure had felt good.

Up ahead of him, a couple was saying goodbye. The girl leaned over and kissed the guy as gently as a butterfly lands on a flower. Tom stopped for a second, stunned. He could feel that kiss. He could feel it because he remembered it. That was the way Elizabeth had kissed him in his dream. In his dream, he was taking her to the Homecoming dance and he'd arrived at her door with a single red rose. Red for passion.

Next to the way Elizabeth had looked, the rose had looked like a weed, but she'd taken it as though it were the most beautiful gift in the world. And then she'd kissed him. Softly. Tenderly. As though her lips had always been intended for his.

Giving himself a shake, Tom started to move forward, but once again he was stopped in his tracks. Just coming out of the athletes' dorm was Elizabeth herself. She must have been working on their story. The happiness he'd felt in his dream was nothing compared to the way the sight of her in the flesh made him feel.

Danny's words came back to him. *God forbid Tom Watts should ever feel happy.* Maybe Danny was right. Maybe a little bit of happiness wasn't out of the question. Maybe he really should ask Elizabeth Wakefield to the Homecoming ball.

"Hey, Elizabeth!" Tom called. "I just—"

She steamed right past him. If she'd been going any faster, he might not even have noticed the tears in her eyes. Instantly he knew that she hadn't been in the dorm because of the story. She'd been there because of her ex-boyfriend, Todd Wilkins. There was no other explanation; not at this time of day, not in a state like that. How could he have fooled himself, even for just a few minutes? He wouldn't have had much of a chance with a woman like Elizabeth anyway. What chance did he have when she was still in love with someone else?

If he'd been alone, Tom would have banged his head against a wall. What a jerk he was to get suckered in by happiness—by hope. There was no such thing as being happy. You were happy for a few minutes, and then something went wrong and it was taken away. He should have learned that by now.

I was right all along, Tom thought as he gloomily resumed his walk to the station. *It's me. I don't deserve to be happy. Not anymore.*

Winston stood in the kitchen area of the Oakley Hall common room, studying the instructions on a container of instant bean soup.

"Just add boiling water," he read, "and in two minutes you will have a nutritious and delicious meal."

He put a pan of water on the stove and turned it on. He opened the container and gave it a sniff. It didn't smell either nutritious or delicious. It just smelled dry. He knew that the cafeteria was serving one of his favorite meals tonight, fried chicken and corn bread, but he couldn't face it. It was Candy's birthday and everyone on the floor had chipped in to buy a cake and ice cream. The girls expected him to eat with them tonight, but if he did, every Sigma in the room would want to eat with them too. They didn't wait to be asked anymore; they just pulled up a chair and joined right in. *Love me, love my frat brothers,* Winston thought sourly.

The worst thing, though, was that he'd really been looking forward to Candy's birthday dinner, because Denise would be there. He'd lain awake half the night, wondering how he could engineer it so he could sit next to her. But just as he was imagining Denise leaning against him, helpless with laughter at his sparkling wit, he'd imagined Bill and a posse of Sigmas squeezing in between them, monopolizing the conversation for the rest of the night and annoying all of his dormmates.

"This is what I'm driven to," he muttered to himself as he waited for the water to boil. "Eating dehydrated beans all alone."

"Do you always talk to yourself, or is it just because none of your frat buddies are around to keep you company?"

Winston's heart turned to dehydrated beans. He knew that voice. He heard that voice in his dreams. That was Denise. Hoping he still had the power of speech, he turned slowly. Denise wasn't at the birthday dinner. She was standing in the doorway, dressed in old sweatpants and a flannel shirt, with a container of instant noodles and a bowl in her hand. She looked a little pale.

"What are you doing here?" he asked, too surprised not to show it. "I thought you'd be at Candy's birthday bash. They've got three kinds of ice cream."

Denise made a face. "And I've got three kinds of cramps. I feel like a squad of kick boxers are practicing in my abdomen."

Cramps. Winston knew about cramps. In the days before he lived in an all-female dorm, he hadn't understood about things like cramps and PMS and cellulite, but he'd learned fast. It didn't even embarrass him to talk about it in public anymore. "Gee, that's too bad," he said sincerely. "Maybe you should be lying down. I know Anoushka recommends a heating pad and Mozart."

Denise laughed. "I've been lying down since I got back from my logic class." She held up the plastic bowl. "I thought eating something might make me feel better."

It astounded him. Even though he was alone with Denise, he was still capable of thought. "Why don't you sit down and I'll fix it for you?" He took the container out of her hand. "The water's already boiling," he said, pointing to the stove. "I made more than enough for two."

"You are a sweetheart," Denise said, sitting down at the table with a grateful sigh.

A sweetheart? Winston practically spilled water all over the counter in his excitement.

"You know, I was really annoyed with you the other night, Winnie," Denise said. "I thought we were friends. I couldn't believe you'd rather sit with the Sigmas than sit with me."

The foil lid on the noodles didn't come off as easily as the foil lid on the black beans had. A small explosion of white, wormlike things and yellow powder landed on the stove. "Me?" Winston squeaked, trying to sweep them back into the container without her noticing.

"Yes, *you*. Did you think I didn't see you? I was sure you were going to come over, but then when Bill and his pals showed up, I figured you must have been waiting for them. Some dormmate you are, letting me eat all alone just so you could talk about football with those guys."

"You're wrong, Denise," Winston protested, wincing in pain as scalding water splattered his hand.

She laughed. "Are you trying to tell me that you boys don't talk about football all the time?"

He turned, carrying the two steaming containers, about to tell her that he'd much rather sit with her than sit with the Sigmas. But even in old sweatpants and a flannel shirt Denise Waters was so beautiful that his body went into meltdown—and instant soup went all over the table. Denise screamed.

"That's why I sat with them," Winston babbled, trying to mop up the soup with the sleeve of his shirt. "I didn't want to ruin your meal."

Denise leaned over and plucked a few noodles from his arm. "I've got beef chop suey and lentil soup in my room," she said. "Should we try this again?"

Chapter
Five

It was the sound of Isabella running the shower that woke Jessica up. In her dream, it had still been yesterday and she was lying on the warm sand, beside a warm, gorgeous man, dizzy with love. In reality, it was today and she had to make some excuse to her philosophy professor about missing the seminar, attend three of the most boring classes ever created, *and* talk to Elizabeth about the Thetas. Jessica groaned out loud. As if that wasn't enough, Mike had some sort of business tonight and wouldn't be able to see her. *If only I could just sleep until tomorrow,* she thought as she dragged herself out of bed. *Then tomorrow wouldn't seem so far away.*

She heard her stomach growl and was suddenly aware that she was starving. She'd been so wrapped up in Michael yesterday, she hadn't really eaten anything. Jessica decided to eat before she got dressed. While one Wakefield twin was putting on weight, the other seemed to be shrinking away, she thought as she passed the mirror.

"Cereal," she chanted as she padded into the kitchenette, "toast, coffee, juice, and condoms."

Condoms? Jessica froze with her hand on the refrigerator door. What had made her say condoms?

Slowly her eyes focused on the shining white enamel in front of her. There were the usual magnets and notes on the door . . . And taped right in the center was a page from a magazine. A young couple, obviously in love and obviously very happy, was smiling at her. Above their heads in large, bold letters was the caption: SEX: IF YOU'RE GOING TO HAVE IT, MAKE IT SAFE! CONDOMS ARE FOR YOU, TOO!

It was incredible. Absolutely incredible. Isabella was still in the bathroom, and already she was getting on Jessica's case.

Jessica snatched the clipping, tossed it into the garbage, and wrenched open the fridge. This day was going to be even longer than she'd thought.

"Have a nice day yesterday?" Isabella asked, squeezing past her to start the coffee.

Jessica kept her head in the refrigerator. "Very nice, thank you."

"And the night before?" Isabella went on. "Was that nice too?"

Slowly and carefully, Jessica loaded bread, butter, milk, and jelly into her arms. "It was perfect,"

94

she said, matching Isabella's flat, polite voice. "Absolutely perfect."

Isabella noisily emptied the coffee filter. "Your brother called three times yesterday. He seemed upset. And your sister called twice last night. She seemed pretty upset too." She noisily poured water into the coffee machine. "I see you got my message."

Jessica straightened up. "If you mean the rather crude advertisement that you stuck on the refrigerator, yes, I got it."

"And what are you going to do about it?" Isabella asked, her eyes meeting Jessica's for the first time.

Jessica swung her golden hair over her shoulder. "I'm not going to do anything about it." She glided past Isabella and put the food on the counter. "It's not any of your business, of course, but for your information, Mike and I are not having sex. The only use we have for condoms is if we decide to have a party and we run out of balloons."

"You're funny, Jess," Isabella snapped. "You're very funny. But it won't be funny if Mike gets you pregnant or gives you AIDS."

Jessica stuck two pieces of bread into the toaster. "We're not sleeping together, Isabella," she explained again with exaggerated patience. "He can't give me anything."

"You spent the night with him, Jess. Maybe you didn't sleep with him this time, but that doesn't mean you won't next time. Believe me, Mike

McAllery doesn't have women spend the night because he's too cheap to buy a teddy bear."

Jessica felt her neck go cold. She wished Isabella would stop referring to Mike's "women" all the time. "But it doesn't mean I'll sleep with him, either."

Isabella sighed. "Jess, get real, will you? *I* saw you two together yesterday. Practically everybody saw you yesterday. It was like Romeo and Juliet meet *The Wild One*."

Jessica reached over Isabella's head for a bowl. "I have kissed people before, you know," she said, jerking the cabinet open. "My boyfriend Sam and I were very passionate and we never had sex."

"You and Sam were in high school, Jess," Isabella snapped back. "You were both kids. And at least one of you was sensible. But this isn't high school, and Mike McAllery isn't a kid." She reached up and slammed the cabinet shut again before Jessica could. "And quite frankly, Ms. Wakefield, I don't think you're being very sensible at the moment!"

Steam hissed out of the coffee machine.

Jessica concentrated on pouring out her cornflakes. "I know what I'm doing, Isabella."

"Do you?"

"Yes," Jessica answered between gritted teeth. "I do."

Isabella came over to her. "Well, just in case you don't know what you're doing as well as you think you do, Juliet, let me give you this with my compliments." She pulled something out of her pocket

96

and dropped it into Jessica's cereal bowl. "My advice is, don't leave home without it."

Jessica looked down as her roommate sailed past her. Sitting on top of the cornflakes was a packet of condoms. Extra strong.

"I mean, really, Isabella," Alison said as they walked across the quad, "you should see some of the girls who can't understand why we don't pledge them. Droids, Isabella. Girls who can't tell silk from viscose." She flicked a microscopic speck of dust from the sleeve of her jacket.

"Gee," Isabella mumbled.

"Girls who *shave* their legs instead of waxing. Girls who aren't even *attractive*!" Shuddering was too violent and obvious an action for Alison, but she wrinkled her nose in distaste.

"Ugh."

"I mean, assuming that they're capable of thought, what do they think, Izzy? We're probably the most prestigious sorority in the entire state. Do they think we got there by taking *dross*? It makes me laugh, Isabella. It just really makes me laugh." To prove that it made her laugh, Alison made a sound somewhere between a toilet backing up and a goose choking.

Isabella nodded and smiled. All Alison needed was a grunt, or a nod, or a smile every minute or so and she was happy to prattle on by herself. And Isabella was happy to let her. This morning, Isabella didn't really feel like talking. She wanted to think.

Despite the lecture she'd given Jessica that morning—and despite the fact that she really did think Mike McAllery was worse news than an outbreak of cholera—seeing her roommate's state of excitement had Isabella thinking of love. Isabella was personable, intelligent, attractive, mature . . . Why hadn't she found someone to fall in love with?

They turned toward the science building and Alison changed the subject. "Did I tell you about my dress for the Homecoming ball?" she asked. "It's going to be stupendous. I mean, not just stunning, not just drop-dead gorgeous, but totally stupendous."

Isabella, who had heard about Alison's dress for Homecoming in some detail every day for the past week, shook her head. She'd been out with some of the most eligible and desirable men at school, but not one of them had made her feel more than mildly interested. Not one of them had made her heart pound, or her body shake, or her mind forget about everything but his smile. The only man who had ever done that was the one who wouldn't give her the time of day.

"Don't you think that's a stupendous idea?"

Isabella looked over to find Alison smiling at her, waiting for an answer. It was so rare for Alison to ask a direct question or expect a direct answer that Isabella had completely lost track of the conversation. Did she think what was a good idea?

Diamond earrings? Dyed-to-match shoes?

"What?"

"Making Elizabeth Wakefield go out with Peter and publicly apologize for being so rude to him at that party." Alison smiled contentedly. "I think even I could accept her commitment to the Thetas if she agreed to that."

Isabella could hardly hide her surprise. "To tell you the truth, Alison," she said calmly, "I don't really think it is such a stupendous idea. Peter behaved like a thug that night. And you know as well as I do that he had something to do with frightening Jessica at the Halloween dance. I really don't think—"

Alison waved aside her objections with one elegantly manicured hand. "I know why you're attacking Peter, Isabella. Don't think I don't."

Isabella bit back a smirk. "You mean aside from the fact that he behaved like a thug?" she asked sweetly.

"It's because of *him*, isn't it?" Alison said. "He and Peter hate each other. You'd be bound to be on *his* side."

Isabella frowned. She was lost again. Now who was Alison talking about?

"You've always been a sap for *him*," Alison continued, sighing at the irrationality of this. "I really don't know why. He's handsome, of course. And such a maverick. But really, Izzy, he is *so* moody and such a troublemaker."

All at once she realized whom Alison was talking about. The one man who had ever really interested Isabella. The one man who had ever disturbed her sleep. And she realized, too, that he must be nearby.

Isabella looked to the left. Tom Watts was just coming out of the WSVU office.

"And of course he isn't really interested in women, is he?" Alison asked, not losing one beat of her conversation. "He isn't really interested in anything except his TV station."

Isabella raised her hand. "Hi, Tom!" she called.

Tom nodded. But his eyes didn't even meet hers.

What I need is some firsthand information, Elizabeth was thinking as she crossed the quad. *Someone who was actually offered money or gifts . . . or someone who knows who was . . .*

Elizabeth had spent most of the morning in the morguelike basement of the journalism building, looking for any information she could find on the teams. She hadn't found any hard proof yet, but she had found suggestions of some pretty suspicious dealings. Illegal presents and arrangements. Unfair privileges. Special exemptions and exceptions made for players. Now she was headed to the station to sort out what she'd found. Knowing how nosy and prying Celine was, she had no intention of leaving anything important in her room.

"Liz! Hey, Elizabeth!"

Elizabeth had been so deep in thought that it

took her a minute to realize that someone was calling her. She looked up. Jessica was running toward her, her eyes sparkling and her cheeks glowing.

"Liz!" Jessica gasped, catching her breath as she drew alongside her. "I can't tell you how happy I am to see you. I've been looking all over for you. In the library . . . in the bookstore . . . I was just going over to Dickenson to see if you were in your room. I really have to talk to you!"

All morning, Elizabeth had been thinking of nothing but the sports scandal. But the sight of her sister put it completely out of her mind. "I really have to talk to *you*," Elizabeth said. "I left two messages for you last night, but you never called back."

Jessica flicked her hair over her shoulder. "That Isabella," she said with a laugh. "She really is one of the worst secretaries I've ever had. Remind me to fire her first thing in the morning."

Elizabeth's expression remained stony. She knew her twin too well to be taken in by the *That Isabella* routine. "Somehow I don't think it's Isabella's fault that you didn't return my calls," she said coolly. Elizabeth had promised herself yesterday that she wasn't going to start shouting at Jessica. That would only make her defensive. They were practically adults now, after all. "I think it's much more likely that the person I have to thank is Mr. McAllery," Elizabeth said.

If Jessica wanted to be an actress, there wasn't a doubt in Elizabeth's mind that her twin could be a star. She was good, there was no denying it. Only the slightest movement in those sea-green eyes gave any indication that she even knew who Mike McAllery was.

"I need to talk to you about the Thetas," Jessica said, as though Elizabeth hadn't even spoken. She slipped an arm through her sister's. "I had a very interesting talk with Alison Quinn the other day, and—"

"And today you're about to have a very interesting talk with me," Elizabeth said, pulling them up short. She could feel her temper rising. "I don't want to talk about the Thetas, Jessica. I want to talk about you and Mike McAllery."

Jessica pulled her arm out of Elizabeth's. Her smile became accusing. "Who told you? Big-mouth Isabella Ricci?"

"No, big-mouth Steven Wakefield." Elizabeth's smile was accusing. "He saw you leaving Mike's apartment at eight thirty in the morning, Jess. He said that Mike McAllery isn't the kind of guy you'd let take your dog out, never mind your sister. He said—"

"What's Steven all of a sudden?" Jessica demanded. "The secret police?" She raised her voice several decibels. "I don't care what Steven says, Elizabeth. It's my life, and I'll do what I want!"

Several people were turning back to look at them as they passed.

"Steven says that Mike threatened him," Elizabeth hissed, trying to shove her off the path so that they could talk more privately.

"Get off me, Liz!" Jessica shoved her back. "Mike did not threaten him. Steven was acting like he was in some macho thriller. Mike was just straightening him out."

Elizabeth dropped her backpack and grabbed Jessica by the arm. "Steven's worried about you, Jess. And so am I. We don't want you to do something you'll regret—"

"Like what?" Jessica yelled, pushing her away. "Like sleep with the man I love?"

"Jessica!" Elizabeth wished she could understand why it was *her* face that went red and not her sister's. She made another grab for Jessica's arm, but Jess was already stalking away. "Jessica, you can't love this man. You don't even know him."

Jessica stopped dead and turned around. Several people bumped into each other trying not to bump into her.

"Then you and Steven can't hate him, Elizabeth," Jessica said in a loud, clear voice. "Because you don't know him, either."

Jessica had felt confused already about whether or not she should sleep with Mike; the last thing she needed was Elizabeth getting into the discussion. She knew her sister too well to think that the argument would stop here. Isabella Ricci might tape condom ads to the refrigerator, but Elizabeth

Wakefield would follow her around like a guilty conscience and never let up.

Maybe I should just go ahead and sleep with him, Jessica was thinking as she stormed back to her suite. *Everybody's already treating me like I'm some kind of fallen women. Everybody acts like it would be such a crime.*

Music was blaring out of dorm windows; people were shouting and laughing as they basked in the sunny afternoon. But Jessica hardly heard it. Instead she heard the disapproving voices of her family and friends. *Don't make love to him,* the voices were saying. *Whatever you do, don't let him touch you.* Except Isabella's voice was saying, *Take the condoms, Jess. If you won't say no to sex, then at least make it safe.*

Eyes blazing, Jessica steamed across the lawn of her dorm. She'd always known that there were two kinds of people in the world. There were people like her sister, who were reliable and cautious, who obeyed the rules and did what they were told. And then there were people like Jessica, who wanted to live life, not just follow the instructions. People who didn't do what they were told. People like Mike.

Everyone thought Mike was no good for her, that she should give him up. Isabella, Denise, Steven, Elizabeth . . . Jessica flew past a gardener trimming the hedge outside her dorm. If she asked him, he'd probably tell her to dump Mike too.

But what did any of them know about Mike?

Nothing. Nothing at all. They looked at him and saw a hard-edged, street-wise guy with a wild streak that scared them.

Jessica entered the suite like a hurricane, throwing her books on the table with a crash. She was confused about whether or not she should sleep with Mike, but she wasn't confused about what she felt for him. He was tough on the outside but gentle on the inside. He could make her laugh and also make her cry. Mike's wild streak didn't scare Jessica; it made her feel alive.

She marched into the bedroom and flung herself on her bed. The voices were getting louder, and the loudest was Isabella's. *What about the other women?* Isabella's voice was saying. *He's a womanizer, Jess. God knows what else he does, but I do know that. He's not a one-woman man. He'll break your heart.*

"You're wrong," Jessica said out loud. "If he's had a lot of women, it's just because he hadn't found the *right* woman yet."

Suddenly another voice drowned out Isabella's. It was Mike's. *You're my baby,* Mike said tenderly. *My little girl . . . And I'm your man . . .*

Her heart pounding, Jessica reached under her pillow and removed the package of condoms. Maybe Mike had finally found the right woman.

She knew she'd find him here. Celine stood in the doorway of the coffeehouse, her eyes fixed on a figure sitting at the back by himself. Other people

105

went to the snack bar or the student center during the day; places where it was light and full of noise, but not William White. He liked it here, where it was dark and subdued. He was the man who was always in the back room at parties and meetings; in the corners, in the shadows.

Celine studied his fine, pale face and those secretive eyes. If she were the kind of girl who believed in the devil, she would have no trouble believing that William was at least his cousin.

She saw the ice-blue eyes flicker as he lifted his cup. He'd seen her. He'd seen her, but of course he wouldn't show that he had. He wouldn't wave to her or beckon her over like a normal person would.

That's all right, William, Celine said to herself. She took a deep breath and hugged her books against her chest. *Because you are not only about to see me, you are about to invite me to the Homecoming ball.* She knew that he was planning to ask Elizabeth. Not because he'd said as much to her, of course. But because he'd asked where Elizabeth had been the last day or two; he hadn't seen her around. He thought she might have gone away. Celine, remembering the rose, took this to mean that he'd been looking for Elizabeth. He was getting ready to ask her out.

William didn't look at her until she was sitting beside him. "Oh, I can't tell you how happy I am to see a friendly face!" Celine gushed, flashing him one of her biggest smiles.

106

He actually smiled back, a thin-lipped smile that curled at one corner. She wasn't sure if he was smiling because he was glad to see her or if he was smiling at some private joke.

"I just couldn't stand it in that room one more minute," she hurried on. "That girl is driving me crazy with talk about the Homecoming ball."

One blond eyebrow rose a fraction as he sipped his espresso.

"Who should she go with? What should she wear? What should they do after the dance? I finally had to say to her, 'Elizabeth, honey, I am *not* your fairy godmother. You are free to do as you please.'" Celine heaved a long-suffering sigh. "Thank heavens she's finally decided who she's going with. At least I don't have to listen to the list of her admirers anymore."

Something that could have been emotion flashed through the dead blue eyes. He put down his cup so softly it might have been made of tissue. "So is this your roundabout way of letting me know that Elizabeth has a date for Homecoming, Celine?" His voice was as soft as tissue as well.

Celine was all innocence. "I thought you might like to know, William," she said. She beckoned for the waitress. "I thought that was our understanding. That I . . . let you know."

"And with whom would this date be?"

Celine shrugged. "I don't have a telepathic mind, Mr. White. I can't even keep track of all the names. It could be one of several."

He stared into the dark depths of his cup for several seconds, considering.

"And what about you?" he asked at last. "Do you have a date for the Homecoming ball?"

Celine laughed. "Of course I do. As it happens, I'm going with—"

"Cancel it." He pushed back his chair and got to his feet.

She looked up at him, her eyes flashing in outrage. "But William, I can't just—"

"Cancel it," he repeated. "You're going with me."

There was a satisfied smile on Celine's beautiful face as she watched him leave the coffeehouse. William White might be the cousin of the devil, but that didn't mean he was the only one with relatives in hell.

I'm Alex, now, not Enid. I'm beautiful, I'm popular, I'm going to be pledged to the biggest sorority on campus, and I have the most gorgeous, generous, and incredible boyfriend in the entire universe. She looked around the exquisite new bistro where Mark had insisted on taking her, Todd, and Lauren to lunch to celebrate passing his big physics exam. It was a little weird, hanging out with Todd and Lauren when she was so used to hanging out with Todd and Elizabeth, but it was a weirdness she was getting used to. After all, things changed and people changed. She'd changed too. *I have to be dreaming,* she thought. *This can't be my life.*

"The sky's the limit as far as I'm concerned," Mark said. He squeezed Enid's hand under the table. "The four of us are going to have the greatest time at the Homecoming ball since man invented parties."

Todd laughed. "I'm with you, Gathers. The sky's the limit. This is the first college Homecoming I've ever been to, and I want to have the time of my life."

"Then it's decided," Mark said. "Dinner at Da Vinci's first, and then on to the dance." He grinned. "With a little bit of luck, my new Explorer will have arrived by then and we can really go in style."

Lauren turned to Enid. "What are we going to do with these guys, Alex?" she asked. "I think they're spoiling us."

Enid thought so too. She knew that Todd's family was pretty comfortable, though not so comfortable that they could put Todd through college without noticing how much it was costing. But she hadn't thought that Mark was particularly well-off at all—not new car and expensive restaurants well-off. She looked from Mark to Todd. They didn't look worried. Their athletics grants must be better than she'd thought.

Enid leaned across the table and gave Mark a kiss. "I think we're going to have to find some way of spoiling them back," she said with a laugh.

* * *

"Winston Egbert! We know you're in there! Open this door!"

Winston stared warily at the door as the knocking became harder and more insistent. Why did he always find himself hiding from people?

"Winnie! What do you want us to do? Break down the door?"

Winston groaned. This was even worse than being harassed by the Sigmas.

"If you don't let us in, we're going for Maia. She'll be on our side in this. She's got the key!"

With the enthusiasm of a man about to open the cage of a starving tiger, Winston forced himself up from the bed.

On the other side of his door were Anoushka and Debbie, and they were mad. They'd been chasing Winston around campus all day, trying to tell him just how mad they were, but he'd been able to give them the slip each time. When they'd seen him coming out of English, he managed to duck into the boys' gym. When they'd spotted him in the cafeteria, he'd abandoned his meal and slipped out while they were still getting their lunch. They'd almost had him cornered in the snack bar, but he'd cleverly escaped through the window of the men's room, even though it had meant tearing one of his favorite shirts.

But now there was no escape. If he jumped out this window he wouldn't just rip his clothes, he'd break both his legs. How was he going to run away from them with two broken legs?

Winston counted to three and opened the door.

The two of them were standing there with their arms folded across their chests and disgusted expressions on their faces. Winston's mother was neither incredibly beautiful nor a college student, as Anoushka and Debbie both were, but for an instant they reminded him an awful lot of Mrs. Egbert.

Winston smiled. "Noush! Deb! What a pleasant surprise."

"Cut the crap, Winnie," Anoushka ordered, sweeping past him. "You know why we're here."

"That's right," Debbie said, stepping on his foot as she marched into the room. Normally the most polite of girls, she didn't even bother saying she was sorry.

"We'd like an explanation, Winnie," Anoushka said, turning to face him.

"And then we'd like an apology," Debbie added. "Preferably public."

Winston looked from one to the other. "Explanation? Apology?"

"Don't try to get out of this, you little weasel," Anoushka snarled.

"Weasel?" Winston was genuinely shocked. "Anoushka, how can you call me a weasel? You like me. I'm your friend."

"That was before you told Tony Calavieri I'd go out with him." She shuddered. "Tony Calavieri!

Winnie, how could you? He's practically a Neanderthal. He doesn't think women should have the vote."

Winston shut the door. There was a good chance that he'd end this conversation on his knees, begging for forgiveness. He didn't need an audience.

"Anoushka, I swear to you, I never told Tony you'd go out with him. He asked me if I thought you'd go out with him, and I said maybe."

Anoushka was glaring. "You expect me to believe that?"

Winston ran his fingers through his hair. "Okay, okay. So that wasn't exactly how it happened. That's not the exact, literal truth." He looked to Debbie for some sympathy, but she was glaring at him too.

"So what is the exact, literal truth?" Anoushka demanded.

He looked at the floor. "Tony asked me to ask you if you'd go out with him, and I sort of said that you said you would."

"You see!" She grabbed an eraser from his desk and threw it at him. "And you call yourself my friend!"

"You hypocrite," Debbie growled. "You arranged to meet me in the library this morning and then you never showed up. Jeff Cross showed up! I can't believe you played a cheap trick like that on me, Winston. Jeff isn't even a Neanderthal. He's the missing link. He couldn't open a milk carton if it didn't come with instructions!"

"Ladies! Ladies! Please, I can explain."

They plopped down on the bed as though they'd been dropped. "So, go ahead. Explain."

Winston explained. He explained about the pressure the Sigmas were putting him under because he lived in a female dorm, how they used subtle threats to make him do favors for him. How they dogged his footsteps. How they wouldn't leave him alone.

"At first I thought it was just that they liked me, you know. They were so friendly and everything. But it's gotten worse and worse. Now I'm afraid that if I don't go along with them, they'll not only dump me from the fraternity, they'll probably dump me over a cliff, too."

"So what if they dump you from their stupid fraternity?" Anoushka demanded. "You don't need them. They're a bunch of morons."

Winston wasn't so sure. Maybe the girls in his dorm had a low opinion of Sigma brothers, but they were still the big men on campus to everybody else. And a big man on campus was what he wanted to be. Besides, there was the other consideration.

"What about the cliff?" Winston asked. "It doesn't upset you that you might have to visit me in the hospital?"

A look passed between the two girls. Anoushka shrugged. "We'll think about it," Debbie said.

Chapter
Six

Elizabeth looked at her watch as she left the athletics office. She'd gotten so involved in listening to Coach Sanchez's reminiscences that she'd completely lost track of the time. Coach Sanchez might not want Tom Watts hanging around asking questions, but he didn't seem to mind Elizabeth Wakefield. As soon as she'd said that she was thinking of doing a piece for the school paper about the importance of sports in campus life, he'd leaned back, put his feet on his desk, and started talking.

He talked about what a loss it had been to the school when Tom Watts quit football. "When I got here, Tom was the best SVU had," Coach Sanchez said. "Heck, he was the best anybody had. The rest of the athletes here were no better than second string. When Tom left, it demoralized everyone, not just the football players. That's when I knew I had to get tough." He told her how he and his staff had turned the SVU athletics department from a third-rate embarrassment no professional scout worth his expenses would even bother to look at into a seedbed for the major teams in every field and every division. "Not that I did it alone," Coach Sanchez kept saying. "I like to give credit where credit is due. This has been a team effort in every sense of the word."

He was full of amusing stories and colorful anecdotes. "Don't forget to mention the time Quemada left his new camera on the bus in Dallas. Chased it five blocks before he caught it." He leaned over to make sure she was getting it down. "You know who I mean, right? He's the one everyone's betting will be snatched up by the NFL when he graduates."

He had lots of useful advice for anyone wanting to put together an award-winning athletic department. "Go for the gold, that's the secret. Just go for the gold. Don't fool around with guys who might be *good* if you work their butts off. Concentrate on the guys who will be *great* if you work their butts off. Then you have a chance."

He kept calling her "angel." "You should try out for the cheerleaders, angel," he'd said more than once. "You've got the sort of looks that really gets the boys' blood moving."

"I'd like to get *his* blood moving," Elizabeth mumbled to herself as she cut across the grass. She was supposed to have met Enid for lunch ten minutes ago.

115

Once she'd reached the main quad, she started to run. *I don't understand why the pounds aren't falling off me*, she was thinking as she raced along. *Never mind how hard I'm working right now and the fact that most of what I eat tastes like cardboard. Between the stress of living with Celine and worrying about Jess, I should be burning up calories by the millions.*

But she wasn't. Elizabeth pounded down the path toward the coffeehouse. This morning she'd weighed herself on Nina's scale and she'd actually put on half a pound. Half a pound! Nina said it must be water. "Water doesn't weigh all that much," Elizabeth had said.

She was still thinking about that half pound when she plowed into someone coming from the opposite direction. They crashed to the ground in a shower of papers and books.

"I'm so sorry," Elizabeth apologized, pulling herself up with as much dignity as she could manage. "I'm really sorry. I didn't even see you. I guess I wasn't paying attention—"

"I guess you weren't." He pulled a leaf from her hair. "It isn't exactly flattering, though, that you didn't even see me."

Elizabeth flushed. She might not have noticed him before, but she noticed him now. He had been almost this close when he handed her the rose in the library, but that hadn't been in daylight. In daylight everything about him looked too perfect to be real—especially that smile.

"On the other hand," he went on, "'there is no such thing as accident, there is only will and chance.'"

"You're quoting," Elizabeth said, smiling back. There had been a time when the way he looked at her made her nervous. It wasn't making her nervous now, but it was making her wish that she'd worn something a little nicer today. It was definitely making her wish that she hadn't gained that half a pound.

"Maldono," he said, picking up one of the books she'd dropped. *Poem to a Lover.* He turned the thin volume over. "It's not in this collection. It's in *Memories and Dreams.* You reading this for a class?"

Elizabeth shook her head. "No, for pleasure."

His eyes went from the book to her. "Not many people read Maldono anymore," he said. "Especially not for pleasure." He smiled. "I think they find her poems a little too much work to be considered fun, but she's always been one of my favorites."

"Mine, too." She couldn't seem to stop looking into those glass-blue eyes. "I like that she's so hard to pin down."

"'I saw you that first morning, walking with your friends. I stopped in the middle of doing something. There was sunlight on the trees and on your hair. Maybe you laughed and looked my way. Maybe you spoke. Maybe it was only a dream.'"

"'Remembering,'" Elizabeth answered immediately.

"I see you know your stuff." He extended his hand. "And I'm William. William White."

"Elizabeth Wakefield," she answered, but she had the feeling he knew that already.

"Maybe you'd like to go for a coffee or something," he said, still holding her hand. "It is lunchtime."

She almost said yes—and then she remembered. "Oh, no! Lunch!" She yanked her hand away and started frantically retrieving her things. "I'm late. I'm sorry, I really have to go."

When they were both on their feet again, he gave her back her book. "Nice bumping into you," he said. "Maybe we can do it again sometime."

"Don't jump down my throat, man." Danny reached into the bag he'd brought into the news office and handed Tom his sandwich. "All I wanted to know was whether you were thinking of asking Elizabeth to Homecoming. It wasn't armed assault; it was just a question."

"And I gave you an answer."

Danny grinned. "No, you didn't, you gave me an attitude."

Tom refused to look into that concerned and friendly smile. He concentrated on unwrapping his sandwich. It was beginning to seem to Tom that no matter how hard you tried to keep people at a distance, there was always one or two who had a way of sneaking up close.

He could feel Danny watching him.

"So why don't you ask Elizabeth to Homecoming?" Danny persisted. "You know you like her. You're always telling me what a terrific reporter she is. How much you enjoy working with her."

Just because Tom had made a few positive comments about Elizabeth, Danny was always bringing her name up lately. Why couldn't he understand that the only passion between Tom and Elizabeth was for the truth?

"Working is the key word here," Tom said. He picked a shred of lettuce from his shirt. "We work together and that's it. Just because Elizabeth and I make a good team at the station doesn't mean I want to dance with her, Danny."

Danny bit into his burger. "So what happened? You asked her and she turned you down?"

Tom felt like banging his head on his computer. He used to be so good at hiding his feelings, but ever since his first glimpse of Elizabeth Wakefield he'd been getting less good. He might as well hang his heart around his neck on a piece of ribbon.

Tom gave up and looked at his friend. "No, Daniel," he said with mock patience, "she did not turn me down."

"So what, then? She's already going with somebody else?"

Tom helped himself to a handful of Danny's french fries. "What are you all of a sudden, Miss Lonely-Hearts?"

"No, I'm just your best friend. And I sense a new restlessness and moodiness in you lately, Tombo. Different than your usual restlessness and moodiness." Danny picked up his iced tea. "So if she's not going with somebody else, why don't you ask her?"

"Because she probably is going with somebody else, all right, Danny? Is that good enough for you? Can we stop now?"

"But you don't know for sure that she has a date—"

"Danny!" Tom threw his sandwich down on the desk. "Has it ever occurred to you that Elizabeth might not want to go to the dance with me?"

Danny took his second burger out of the bag. "Has it ever occurred to you that she might?"

"So what have you been up to, Alex?" Elizabeth asked as the waitress set her salad plate in front of her.

She shrugged. "Oh, not much. You know, the usual."

Enid almost wished that she'd given up waiting for Elizabeth and left the coffeehouse when she had the chance. Elizabeth seemed distracted, and anyway, what were they supposed to talk about now that they'd drifted so far apart? They'd already gone through classes and the weather and the latest movies. The things that Enid really wanted to talk about—Mark and her wonderful new life—all involved either the Thetas or Todd. And she couldn't mention those things to Elizabeth without starting an argument or hurting her feelings.

"Not much? What about Homecoming? You must be getting ready for that. It's practically all anybody talks about anymore."

Enid perked up. Maybe this wasn't going to be so difficult after all. Maybe Elizabeth had a big date for the dance and wouldn't even notice that Alex and Mark were doubling with Todd and Lauren.

"It is pretty thrilling, isn't it?" she asked, letting her excitement show. "I mean, our first college Homecoming! Mark's taking me to Da Vinci's for dinner first and everything. I just know it's going to be the best night of my entire life."

Elizabeth gave her a quizzical look. "Da Vinci's? That's pretty fancy, isn't it? I thought a family of South American peasants could eat for a week on what a bowl of soup costs at that place."

Enid used to admire Elizabeth for her seriousness and sense of purpose, but at the moment she found it slightly annoying. She didn't have to worry about world starvation *all* the time, did she?

"What about you?" Enid asked, hoping to change the subject. Her mind was on party dresses and romantic evenings, not poor people. "Who are you going to Homecoming with?"

"Me?" Elizabeth stabbed a lettuce leaf. "I'm not going to Homecoming, Alex. I don't think I could stand spending the whole night watching Todd with someone else."

Enid grabbed her fork. It was time to put something in her mouth besides her foot. "Did I tell you Mark's getting a new car?" she asked, racing for yet another subject. "An Explorer. It is so neat, Liz. Wait'll you see it. He's having it custom painted and ground lights put on and everything."

The quizzical look came back. "A new car?"

There was something about the way Elizabeth said *A new car*? that Enid didn't like. Any second now she was going to tell her that a family of South American peasants could buy shoes for the next two years with what it cost Mark for an oil change.

"But did I tell you the best news?" Enid asked, racing on. "Mark thinks he can take me with him when the team goes on their winter break. Won't that be wonderful? Last year they went to—"

"Santa Fe," Elizabeth said. "To a dude ranch."

As eager as she was to keep the conversation going, and going away from South America and Todd Wilkins, Enid paused. "How did you know that?"

"I don't know." Elizabeth bit into a carrot stick. "I guess somebody must have told me."

"But it's great, don't you think?" Enid steamed on. "Mark thinks they might even go to New Orleans this year. Don't you think that's wonderful? New Orleans?"

Elizabeth chewed thoughtfully. "I'll tell you what I think, Alex," she said at last. "I think it's pretty amazing."

Maia banged on the desk. "Okay, ladies and Winston, settle down, will you? We want to get this floor meeting started before dawn if we can."

There was a flurry of activity as the latecomers found seats.

"Winnie, what *are* you doing?"

Winston, the latest of the latecomers, had been just about to sit down next to Candy when he saw Denise on the other side of the crowded room.

"I just—I was—" Every eye was on him. He couldn't very well say that he'd changed his mind, he wanted to sit next to Denise. "I forgot something in my room—"

"Winnie!"

Maia was giving him a look his mother sometimes gave him. It wasn't without affection, but it wasn't without violence, either.

Half up and half down, Winston stared back at her. "What?"

"Don't you think it would be nice if you just sat down and let us get started, since this meeting is about you?"

"What?"

There was a ripple of laughter around him. Suddenly Winston wished he'd gone to the movies with Bruce Patman and a couple of the other

Sigmas after all. Was she serious? This meeting wasn't supposed to be about *him*, it was supposed to be about keeping the bathroom clean and noise down and stuff like that.

"But I thought this was just a regular floor meeting," Winston said. "Anoushka said—" He glared at Anoushka.

"If I told you the truth, you would have come up with some excuse for not being here," Anoushka said.

Winston started to deny this ridiculous accusation, but Maia cut him off. "Sit down, Winnie! We all have other things to do, you know. We don't want to spend the whole night talking about you."

He didn't particularly want to spend any of the night talking about him, but he sat down obediently.

"Okay," Maia said. "We all know that there have been a few extra problems in our lives since Winnie moved on our floor."

"Problems in blue jackets," someone commented.

Everyone but Winston started to giggle.

"It's true," Anoushka said. "It's been like the invasion of the Sigmas around here ever since Winnie got in with them. And it's driving most of us nuts."

"It's driving all of us nuts," Maia said. "You can barely walk into the dorm without tripping over one of Winston's frat brothers."

Candy put a hand on Winston's shoulder. "It's not that we have anything *against* the Sigmas . . ."

"Oh, I don't know about that," Debbie said. "I hold Jeff Cross against them."

"What about Bill, the man of a thousand hands?" Denise asked.

"What about Bruce Patman?"

"He's nothing compared to Peter the Great."

"Peter the Great Pain in the Butt."

"Let's not forget—"

"Ladies!" Maia was banging on the desk again. "Ladies, please. We don't have to go through all the ugly details. We know the ugly details. They're always asking us out. The only thing that concerns us tonight is the fact that the Sigmas think that just because Winnie lives with us, it gives them some special rights."

Anoushka nodded. "It's like they think because one of their friends lives on a certain piece of land, they're all allowed to hunt on it, never mind what the peaceful natives think."

Winston looked around at the roomful of intelligent, attractive, and angry faces. He wasn't so sure about them being peaceful natives. They looked more like an uprising to him.

"So what's the solution?" asked Tamara. "Is Winnie going to depledge the Sigmas?"

Winston started to choke. Candy pounded him on the back.

"Debbie and I thought of that," Anoushka said.

125

"But it would upset Winnie too much."

Winston threw her a grateful smile.

"So what are we going to do?" Tamara demanded.

Anoushka raised her right arm in the air, making a fist. "We're going to arm the natives."

"Steven, will you please get away from that window? You're acting like a jealous boyfriend."

Steven was standing with his back to the room, peering through the crack in the curtains at the street below. "I am not acting like a jealous boyfriend, Billie. I'm acting like a concerned older brother."

Billie sighed. He could picture the expression on her face. Her eyebrows were drawn together, and her mouth was somewhere between a pout and a sneer. He could picture this expression because he'd been seeing it a lot lately. Ever since the morning he found Jessica kissing Mike McAllery on the stoop.

"Steven . . . come on. I know you're concerned, but Jessica is a big girl now. You can give her advice, but she's going to have to make her own mistakes, just like everyone else."

Steven swung around. "I can't believe you, Billie. I really can't. Mike McAllery is not a *mistake*. Joining the wrong sorority or shaving your head and piercing your nose, *those* are mistakes. Next to them, Mike McAllery is World War III."

"And you are Bozo the Clown." She marched

over and shut the curtains. "This is ridiculous, Steven. You cannot spend the rest of your life waiting for Jessica to come back to Mike's. Dinner's ready and I'm hungry. Let's sit down and eat."

He parted the curtains again. "I'm not hungry."

"Steven!"

"I just have this feeling, Billie. I'm sure she's coming here tonight." He looked into the dark blue eyes that had given him so much sympathy and understanding since they'd met. She thought he was going insane. "Okay, so maybe you think it's crazy, but you have to remember how close my family is. And intuitive. Elizabeth and Jessica can practically read each other's minds."

"Nobody could read your mind," Billie said. "Everything in there is gobbledygook."

Steven threw his hands in the air. "What is it with you women? How can you be so intelligent and still be fooled so easily by a good-looking guy? Why can't you see how dangerous he is?"

Billie put her arms around him. "Steven, Michael McAllery is not Al Capone. I know he has a reputation for being a little wild, and I know there are a lot of women in and out of that apartment—"

"A lot of women! You'd think he was running a hair salon!"

"Steven, that does not make him a criminal."

"Have you seen that bike, Billie? Have you seen that car? Drug dealers drive cars like that. Over-sexed rock stars ride bikes like that."

Billie took her arms away. "Okay, Steven, if you want to spend the night standing at the window, then go right ahead. I'm going to eat."

He put his face to the glass again.

"Steven."

"What?"

"Can I ask you just one little question?"

"I thought you were hungry. Isn't there something burning on the stove?"

She ignored him. "I want to know why, if you're so concerned about Jessica, you don't just tell your parents. If it's anyone's responsibility, it's theirs, not yours."

He turned to her in amazement. "Tell my *parents*? Are you joking? You know what my parents are like. They could never handle something like this, Billie. They always blow things out of proportion."

Jessica's palms were sweating and her heart was pounding as though she'd run all the way from the dorm. Halfway there she'd started imagining what Isabella, Steven, and Elizabeth would say if they knew where she was going in her new silk sheath and matching underwear. Halfway to Mike's, Isabella's condoms in her bag, their arguments started making sense. He was too old and experienced. He was only using her. She knew nothing about him. She was letting her hormones rule her head.

She'd made herself so nervous that she'd almost turned around and gone back to the campus. But then she'd remembered what it felt like to have Mike's arms around her and his lips on hers.

Now that she was here, in his building, only feet away from him, the nervousness returned. *What if I've got the wrong night?* she asked herself as she stopped in front of his door. *What if he forgot? What if he had to go out for some emergency? What if he's with someone—* She closed her eyes. She wasn't even going to let herself think about that one. She counted to three, and then pressed the bell.

Mike answered on the second ring.

Her brother and her sister and her roommate were wrong. She was in the right place, with the right man. Jessica felt so happy at the sight of him that she thought her heart would explode.

"How's my baby tonight?"

His hair was hanging loose, and he was wearing black jeans and a long-sleeved T-shirt the same color as his eyes. If there had ever been another man as beautiful as this, it must have been a very long time ago. She didn't so much fall as float into his arms.

"She's fine now," Jessica whispered, all her fears and nervousness evaporating as she found his lips. "She's just fine."

Jessica wasn't sure how long they stood there kissing. It might have been a few minutes; it might have been a few days. Time didn't seem to have much meaning when she was with Mike. Not time or anything else.

Mike pulled away when he heard footsteps

129

coming down the stairs. "I'm not usually paranoid, but that might be your brother with a gun," he joked. "Maybe we'd better continue this inside."

"Inside sounds great to me." She laughed as he lifted her in his arms.

"I hope you're hungry," he said, setting her on her feet in the dining alcove and slipping off her jacket. "I've been slaving over a hot stove all day for you."

"Oh, Mike!"

Jessica looked around her. There were glowing candles and headily scented flowers all through the alcove and in the living room. Music played softly in the background—not the corny romantic music her parents liked, but raunchy, sensuous blues. The table was covered with a black cloth and set for two. On one of the plates was an orchid tinted the blue-green of the sea.

This can't be real, she told herself. *I must be in a movie or a fairy tale . . .* Mike came up behind her, cocooning her in his arms, his kisses like fireflies dancing on her skin. *Or in a dream . . .*

"I made salmon mousse to start," he whispered, the fireflies moving gently down her neck. "And chicken and mushrooms in wine and herbs for the entreé." The fireflies started a tango across her back. "And for dessert—"

She turned to let the fireflies warm the hollow of her neck. "Maybe we can skip dessert . . ." she whispered.

Once more Mike lifted her in his arms. "Maybe we can start with it," he said.

"My granny always said that it's patience that separates the saints from the sinners," Celine was saying as she studied her eyebrows in the mirror over the sink. She leaned forward and pulled a few imperfectly placed hairs from each eyebrow with her gold-tipped tweezers. "But to tell you the truth, I think I am beginning to run out of patience."

Celine turned to the girl at the sink on her right. "I've tried my best, but there are limits, aren't there? I mean, if the planet can run out of rain forests, a person can run out of patience, can't she?"

The girl, whose name was something like Jem, nodded sympathetically. "Of course there are limits," she said. "The idea of sharing a room with someone is that you *share*. Elizabeth must have missed that day of kindergarten."

"It's true," the girl on Celine's left said. "If one person's doing all the giving and the other's doing all the taking, then you've got a problem."

Celine looked sadly at her reflection. "I don't want to be unfair to Elizabeth. I'm sure she has her reasons—I mean, who knows what dreadful things she's suffered in her life . . ." Celine's reflection looked sadly back at her. "I've tried. The Lord knows I've tried, but maybe I haven't been understanding enough . . ."

The girl on Celine's left splashed water on her

131

face and looked over. "Don't start making excuses for her," she advised. "Admit it. You've got a problem. That's all there is to it."

Celine sighed. "I guess I do have to admit it," she said in a soft, reluctant, saintly voice. "I have got a problem. I am living with a person who thinks only of herself."

"Why don't you talk to her?" asked the girl whose name was maybe Em instead of Jem. "Maybe she just doesn't realize how much she's upsetting you. Sometimes just sitting down and talking really helps."

Celine gave her the smile of a martyr tied to the stake. "Oh, she knows." She shook her head. "I cannot tell you how many times I have tried to talk to her. I even told her I could live with the mess. I could live with her taking my things without asking. I could even get used to her playing her music when I'm trying to study." She smiled again. "But it's the running around all the time I can't handle . . . She's out till all hours, partying and carousing. Sometimes she even brings *boys* back to the room with her. I never know when she's going to burst in or what kind of mood she'll be in. . . ."

The girl on Celine's left finished drying her face. "Oh, I couldn't put up with that either," she said. "I can put up with snoring and weird eating habits, but I couldn't put up with that stuff."

Jem or Em shook her toothbrush in agreement. "Me neither. That's way over the top."

"I know," Celine said with another saintly sigh. "My granny would turn blue and swallow her dentures if she knew what I have to put up with."

"You mean your granny would turn blue and swallow her dentures if she knew how much you lie," said a voice that belonged to neither of the girls at the sinks.

Celine looked into the mirror. Nina Harper had just emerged from one of the shower cubicles and was standing directly behind her, wearing a striped terry-cloth robe and a disgusted expression.

Now, what's your problem? Celine wondered, hiding her frown. She'd been spreading so many rumors about Elizabeth since the beginning of term that she'd been certain she'd turned everyone on their floor against her. She'd convinced them that Elizabeth's shyness was snobbiness and that the reason she had so little to do with the other girls in the dorm wasn't because she thought they didn't like her, but because she didn't like them. Apparently, however, she'd been wrong. Nina Harper had slipped through her net.

"Why, Nina . . ." Celine turned slowly, her eyes wide with innocence and hurt. "I have no idea what you're talking about."

Both whatever her name was and the other girl had stopped their scrubbing and brushing and were staring at Celine.

"Don't you?" Nina threw her towel over her shoulder. "Well, I don't know what you're talking about either," she said. "I happen to be a friend of Elizabeth's, and the person you're describing isn't like her at all."

Inwardly Celine was cursing herself. She'd known, of course, that Nina was a drip like Elizabeth, who was always in the library studying. One might be black on the outside and the other might be white, but inside they were obviously the same color: boring gray. Unfortunately, it had never occurred to Celine that the Dull Duo might actually have started talking to each other.

Outwardly Celine continued to look innocent and hurt. "I think I know Elizabeth a little better than you do," she said sweetly. "I am her roommate, after all."

"And I spend almost every night in the library study room with her," Nina said, just as sweetly.

The other two girls stopped staring at Celine and started staring at Nina.

"So where you get your stories about Elizabeth being out partying all the time is beyond me," Nina continued. "And how you'd know she was out is another question. Anybody who knows you knows that you're never in. I've never been to a party on this campus when you weren't there."

Feeling the eyes on her again, Celine opened her mouth to defend herself, her mind moving fast. Somehow she had to discredit Nina. Because she was always working and didn't really hang out with anyone, Nina wasn't much more popular than

Elizabeth in the dorm. It shouldn't be that hard to make her look like the liar.

"Why are you attacking me like this?" she asked, her voice quavering with emotion. "Is it because you blame my people for slavery? Is that it? Are you mad at me because I come from the South?"

For the first time the hard, disgusted expression left Nina's face. She started to laugh. Quietly at first, and then so loudly that everyone but Celine joined in.

"No, Celine," Nina gasped. "I'm not mad at you because you come from the South. I'm mad at you because you didn't stay there."

Celine was sitting with her feet up on Elizabeth's desk, idly searching through the drawers. The scene in the bathroom had thrown her, but it hadn't discouraged or defeated her. Celine's granny hadn't raised any giver-uppers. Her granny said that it wasn't the early bird who got the worm; it was the bird who hung around from the night before.

"Nothing," Celine murmured, slamming another drawer shut. "She doesn't even take extra bags of sugar from the snack bar."

She knew that Elizabeth hid her diary from her, but she still thought she'd find something just a teensy bit interesting lying around. Something that she could use against her.

Celine yawned. Even if she did find the diary itself, it probably wasn't going to yield any real dirt. Elizabeth had fewer secrets than a goldfish.

She yanked open the bottom drawer. Cigarette ash spilled over Elizabeth's things as Celine rummaged through them. Two unused notebooks. A spare pack of typewriter paper. Extra pens. A brand-new box of staples. Celine yawned again. What could be more boring than a girl who was afraid she might run out of staples in the middle of the night?

She was just about to shut the drawer when she noticed a piece of paper stuck at the back. Never one to overlook the smallest thing, Celine pulled it out.

The crumpled sheet had been torn from a blue-lined pad. There were a few incomprehensible notes scribbled on it in handwriting that was too loose and sloppy to be Elizabeth's. Most of the notes had been crossed out. Celine turned over the page. At the top, in Elizabeth's neat, precise writing, were the words *Illegal Recruitment of Athletes at SVU*. Underneath, also in Elizabeth's handwriting, was an outline for what was obviously an article of some kind.

"Now, what have we here? Don't tell me the Little Princess has a vindictive streak in her?" She laughed gleefully. "Don't tell me she's planning to get even with poor Todd for dumping her for someone else?"

A slow, self-satisfied smile spread across Celine's face like an oil slick on water. She folded the piece of paper and slipped it into her pocket. Maybe Mr. White wouldn't be quite so taken with Little Goody Two Shoes if he knew that she was really a mean and spiteful little witch.

Chapter Seven

Jessica woke up with sunlight pressing against the cloth blinds of the bedroom and Mike's arms around her. Hardly daring to move, she lay there listening to his rhythmic breathing and the steady beating of his heart. There were voices on the street outside and the sounds of traffic hurrying by. It was a normal day. A day just like any other day. Except for one thing. Except for the fact that last night, Jessica had made love for the first time.

Jessica pressed closer to Mike. *This is so weird,* she thought. *It doesn't seem like anything's changed.*

She'd expected to feel different. She was a woman now, a *real* woman, like Lila was. Jessica had always thought that when you became a woman, it was like joining a secret society. And it was true, in a way. She knew things this morning that she hadn't known yesterday morning; she'd experienced things last night that she had never experienced before.

Surely that was supposed to change you, make you and everything else in the world different. But it hadn't; everything felt exactly the same.

Careful not to disturb Mike, Jessica slid from the bed and crossed over to the mirror above the antique dresser. She stared at herself in the glass. She looked exactly the same too. If becoming a woman was like joining a secret society, it was a secret society with no special medallion or handshake, that was for sure.

She bent her head close to her body. Mike's faint aroma still lingered on her skin and in her hair. A little thrill ran through her. Jessica smiled at her reflection. There was no way anyone could look at her and know about the night she'd just spent. Because there was a change in her heart. She might have thought that she was in love with Mike before last night, but now she was sure.

In the mirror Jessica could see his hand searching for her as he slowly opened his eyes. "Baby," he said. "What are you doing way over there?"

Jessica turned and walked over to the bed. "I just wanted to see if I looked any different." She leaned down to kiss him. "You know, to see if I'd changed."

"You have changed," Mike said. He touched her cheek. "You look even more beautiful this morning than you did last night."

"I bet you say that to all the girls," she teased.

Mike made a thoughtful face. "No," he said,

shaking his head in mock seriousness. "Not to all of them."

On any other day, a remark like that would have sunk her into depression, but this morning she knew he was only teasing. She could see it in his deep, dark eyes.

"That's not what you're supposed to say!" Jessica made a movement to punch him, but he caught her arms and pulled her into another kiss.

"So how does my baby feel this morning?" he asked when they finally drew apart. "Or don't you feel like my baby anymore?" he asked with a smile.

"I'll tell you what I feel like," Jessica answered, yanking him off the bed with a laugh. "I feel like a cheese omelette and toast. I'm starving. For some reason, I didn't have any dinner last night."

As far as Isabella was concerned, there were some days that should be skipped altogether. Days when everything was going to go wrong. When you woke up and it was raining, and you'd forgotten to iron the blouse you were going to wear today, and you knew you would have cramps by lunchtime. Days when a girl should stay in bed, not answering the phone or answering the door, just waiting till it was dark and the good television shows came on.

The minute she opened her eyes that morning, Isabella had known that it was going to be one of those days.

"Oh, I don't believe this," she'd groaned out loud as her eyes fell on Jessica's untouched bed.

There wasn't a doubt in Isabella's mind that even after all the good advice and the strong warnings she'd given her roommate, Jessica had decided to sleep with Mike McAllery. And she also knew that Jessica might just as well have walked off a cliff with her eyes wide open and a smile on her face.

Isabella thumped into the bathroom. "Why are women such dopes sometimes?" she asked her reflection.

Her reflection gave her a wry smile. And Isabella forgot about Jessica for a moment as she remembered Tom Watts. Last night he'd been in her dream. She'd been walking across the quad and he'd been coming in the opposite direction. Unlike when she saw him in real life, in her dream he'd been glad to see her. He'd called her "Izzy" and stopped to talk. When he'd left, he'd smiled at her and kissed her on the cheek.

Isabella was still thinking about Tom when there was a knock on the door. She figured Jessica must have forgotten her key. "Just as long as she didn't forget the condoms . . ." Isabella muttered to herself as she hurried out of the bathroom.

But it wasn't Jessica. It was Alison Quinn, dressed all in white and looking as though she'd just come off a dry cleaner's rack. Even her hair looked as though it had been chemically cleaned.

Alison smiled, walking past Isabella and into the

suite as though she lived there. Alison was not a person to wait for invitations.

"I had to pass by here on my way to a Theta breakfast meeting," she said as she sailed into the living room. "You know, to discuss the pledges and that kind of thing." She stood in the center of the room, her eyes straying through the open door to the bedroom. "I thought I might have a word with Jessica about her sister," Alison said. "I'd like to be able to tell my sorority sisters that the matter is under control."

"I think I'll make some coffee," Isabella said brightly. "Would you like some?"

"Where is Jessica?" Alison asked. She glanced at her watch. "It's not even eight. Don't tell me she's gone to a class."

Isabella looked over the counter that separated the kitchenette from the living room. "Milk and sugar?"

But Alison was staring at Jessica's unslept-in bed. "Didn't she sleep here last night?" she asked.

Isabella didn't blink. She'd been at boarding schools and belonged to exclusive clubs and sororities most of her life. She was used to dealing with girls like Alison.

"I guess she stayed at her brother's," Isabella said. "You know Steven Wakefield, don't you? He lives over by Cayuga."

"Her brother?" Alison's eyes met Isabella's. Alison had been dealing with girls like Isabella all

141

her life too. She trusted no one. "Just so long as she is with her brother," she said menacingly. "I mean, I'd hate to think that she was spending the night with Mike McAllery. He isn't exactly our . . . type. I thought she understood that."

Isabella smiled. "You do take sugar, don't you, Alison?" she asked. *You could certainly use it.*

Celine hated the rain, and not just because it made her hair go limp. It was hard to carry on a conversation with someone when you were walking in the rain. Especially if that someone refused to get under your candy-striped umbrella but strode through the downpour so quickly that you practically had to run to keep up with him.

"You know what our girl reporter's up to now?" Celine asked, trying to sound casual despite the fact that she was jogging.

William White glanced over at her. Everyone else wore bright-colored ponchos and parkas in this weather, but not William. He wore a long black canvas coat and a black slouch hat. He looked like he'd just stepped out of a spaghetti Western. He was the cowboy you should never turn your back on. Celine hated him for looking so attractive as much as she hated the rain.

"Girl reporter?" William asked, slowing down just a little.

"Didn't I tell you that Elizabeth started working at the television station? Apparently she was quite the journalist in high school, and now she's decided to go in for television reporting. It's supposed to be a big deal. She's getting special training or something."

William slowed down a little more. "With Tom?" he asked. "Tom Watts?"

There was something about the way he said the name that caught Celine's attention. It wasn't just dislike. William disliked almost everyone, anyway; there was nothing unusual in that. It was that she thought she'd heard the tiniest bit of . . . anxiety in his voice. Celine pushed the idea away. It was ridiculous, of course. William White wasn't afraid of anything. Not even her.

Celine shrugged and the umbrella bobbed. "I really don't know," she answered. "We haven't talked about it at any great length. I guess she's working with Tom. He's the big hotshot reporter there, isn't he?"

William nodded. "Yeah, he's the big hotshot reporter." He was walking beside her now, at her pace, his arm touching hers. "So what's the story Elizabeth's doing?" he asked. "I take it it's not about fall fashions or Homecoming."

"You can bet your last million that it's not about fashion." Celine smiled, sweetly and slyly.

He gave her elbow a squeeze. "So what is it about? You know I hate it when you play games with me, Celine."

Celine pulled away. As beautiful as William was,

he definitely had a lousy temper. "It's about the illegal recruitment of athletes on the SVU campus," she said slowly, pausing for the words to take effect.

"What? It's about what?"

"The illegal recruitment of athletes. You know," Celine explained, "when they give them special privileges and things so they'll come here instead of going somewhere else."

William nodded again. "Oh, is that all." He sounded relieved.

Celine looked at him sharply. *Is that all?* Had he missed the significance of this entirely?

"Well, I'm glad to see you're taking it so calmly," Celine continued. "Because I must say, I was a little shocked myself. I mean, I know Elizabeth and Todd Wilkins aren't together anymore, but I did think it was a little vindictive of her to try to get back at him like that."

William stopped. "Are you saying that Elizabeth's doing this story just to get her old boyfriend in trouble?" he asked.

She looked back at him, innocent as a leaf. "I don't *know* for sure," Celine purred. "But it does seem a little tacky, doesn't it? I mean, to do a story that's going to cause a major scandal when you know your ex-boyfriend is one of the biggest new jocks on campus." She made a helpless, bewildered face. "What do you think? Don't you think it's a little strange?"

He wasn't revolted or outraged. He smiled. "I

think it must mean she doesn't love him anymore."

"This is incredible," Tom said, his voice openly admiring. "Absolutely incredible." He turned to Elizabeth, his eyes shining with excitement. "You've done an amazing job."

Elizabeth flushed at the praise. Coming from Tom, who everyone said gave praise sparingly, if ever, it really meant something. She looked into his eyes.

People always said that the eyes were the windows to the soul, but in Tom's case they were the shutters. His eyes were usually so guarded and wary that it was impossible to guess what was going on in his head, never mind his heart. But right now, his look was so open she almost thought that it wasn't just excitement that made his eyes shine, but pride as well.

"I'm just getting started," she said, forcing her gaze away from Tom's eyes. She pointed to the new outline she'd made for herself. "I still want to talk to alumni; you know, ex-players and team supporters. But also to people who were involved in athletics here before Coach Sanchez remade the department."

He looked up from her notes. "That's brilliant," he said. "If you can show just how systems, expectations, and attitudes have changed, you'll know exactly what you're looking for."

She nodded. "If I can make a comparison, I can

really show what's happened here. As it is, the change has been so gradual that nobody even questions what's been going on."

Tom laughed. It was a sound not often heard in the office of WSVU, but it was a sound that Elizabeth knew she could easily get used to.

They were sitting side by side at Tom's desk, so close that their arms were touching. If she'd leaned toward him just a little she would have felt his breath on her face.

Elizabeth had been with Todd for so long that she'd almost forgotten other men existed. She noticed if someone was attractive, but she didn't think whether or not he was attractive to *her*. That hadn't changed since her breakup with Todd, either. There was such a hole in her life where Todd used to be that she couldn't even begin to think of filling it with someone else.

And yet now she felt these surges of awkward, unexpected emotion she hadn't felt in so long. There was definitely something about Tom . . .

"Professor Sedder said you were exceptional," Tom said with a smile. "But he didn't say just how exceptional."

"He didn't say how exceptional you were, either." Elizabeth just sat there, looking into those wary, intelligent eyes, the color burning her cheeks. She hadn't meant to say that; she hadn't meant to say that at all. Confused, she turned back to her notes.

Tom turned back to her notes too. There was an uneasy silence between them.

"What about Todd Wilkins?" Tom asked suddenly.

Elizabeth dropped her pen. "What?" It was almost as though by thinking about Todd, she'd brought him into the room with them.

Tom leaned down and retrieved the pen for her. "Todd Wilkins," he repeated. "I know you two used to—" His eyes went back to the desktop. "I know you two used to go out." He took a deep breath, carefully choosing his words. "You realize that even from what you've got now, there is a chance Todd might be . . . implicated in all this. I wouldn't want you to—"

"It's not a problem," Elizabeth said quickly. For some reason, she didn't want Tom to think that she was doing this to get back at Todd because she was still so in love with him. "I know Todd really well, and whatever's going on, I'm sure he isn't part of it. He would never do anything that was even a little illegal."

"Right," Tom said, a little shortly. "I just thought—"

"He's one of the most honest people I know," Elizabeth added with a little more emotion than she'd intended. "There's no question about his role in this."

"All right," Tom said. His voice was calm and controlled, but the wary, guarded look was back in his eyes. The mood of excitement and closeness that had passed between them was gone.

"I didn't mean to sound so . . . so bossy," she apologized.

"Don't mention it." He pushed back his chair. "I got the message. George Washington, Abe Lincoln, and Todd Wilkins—the three most honest men America has ever produced." He gave her a businesslike smile. "I wonder if this means Todd Wilkins is going to be the first basketball player in the White House."

Isabella was just about to leave for her first class when the door burst open and Jessica exploded into the suite.

"Guess what?" Jessica said as she threw her things on the couch and collapsed beside them. "Mike's going to take me to the Homecoming ball!" Jessica was almost glowing. "Isn't that wonderful? We're going to be the most fantastic couple there."

Isabella put her books down on the table. She'd promised herself that when Jessica got back from Mike's, she wasn't going to act like a mother hen. She'd vowed that she wasn't going to lose her temper and make a scene. After all, Isabella had been involved in serious relationships herself once or twice. It wasn't as though she couldn't sympathize with her friend.

"I can't wait to see Mike really dressed up,"

Jessica was babbling on. "He'll look so gorgeous, he should be illegal."

Isabella resisted the temptation to say that Mike McAllery probably already was illegal. She took a deep breath, and when she spoke, her voice was pleasant and normal. "Alison Quinn was looking for you," she said. "You missed her by ten or fifteen minutes."

Jessica broke off from wondering out loud whether or not Mike would wear a tux to the dance. "Alison Quinn," she said, looking puzzled. "What did she want? I already know I'm being pledged to the Thetas."

"She wanted to talk to you about Elizabeth. She wants you to tell Elizabeth what she has to do to prove her loyalty to the Thetas."

"I don't know what she has to do," Jessica said, stifling a yawn.

Isabella picked up a pale violet envelope with the silver sorority insignia on it. "You do now," she said, handing it to her.

Isabella watched Jessica reading the note, waiting for her reaction. She'd expected Jessica to be as outraged and horrified as she was, but she'd been wrong. The sea-green eyes looked a little dismayed; that was all.

Jessica tossed the violet notepaper aside as though it were no more than a shopping list. "I'll talk to Liz this afternoon. She's going to take some convincing—I mean, she isn't exactly Peter Wilbourne's biggest fan—but I'm sure she'll come around." She got up and stretched.

"Is that it?" asked Isabella.

"Is what it?"

"Is that all you have to say about it? After the way Peter Wilbourne treated you and Danny, and the way the Sigmas harassed you and Elizabeth, is that all you can say? 'She'll come around'?"

Jessica looked baffled. "What do you want me to say? That I won't join the Thetas because they want my sister to go out with Peter the Creep?"

"No," Isabella said, shaking her head. "I don't want you to drop the sorority, Jess; I just thought you'd be a little angry—you know, that you might stand up to Alison."

"Stand up to Alison—are you nuts, Isabella? The Thetas would drop me in a second if I did that."

"Not necessarily," Isabella argued. "You might convince them to give Elizabeth some other kind of test."

"Might," Jessica said. "And they *might* not." She started toward the bathroom. "Well, it's not a chance I'm willing to take. Joining the Thetas is too important to me."

"Really?" Isabella said. "What about Mike, then? The Thetas don't approve of him either, you know."

Jessica swung around. "I knew it," she said. "I knew you'd get on me about Mike. That's what all

150

this is about, isn't it? It has nothing to do with Elizabeth and the Thetas."

"Of course it has to do with Elizabeth and the Thetas—"

Jessica shook her head defiantly. "No, it doesn't. It's all because I slept with Mike." She made a face. "Well, you don't have to worry, Isabella. I took the condoms with me. I was very careful."

"It's not just your body I want you to be careful about!" Isabella shouted as the bathroom door slammed shut behind Jessica. "It's also your heart!"

Jessica was singing along to the love song playing on her Walkman as she entered Dickenson Hall, the dorm where her sister lived. Her argument with Isabella was already forgotten and her good mood restored. She had more important things to think about than Isabella Ricci or even Alison Quinn. She had Mike McAllery. No matter where she was or what she was supposed to be doing—eating, talking, walking across campus, listening to a lecture on some dead person with an unpronounceable name—it was Mike who filled her thoughts. She couldn't stay in a bad mood when she had him on her mind.

"It's not just for now, it's forever," Jessica sang as she climbed the stairs to Elizabeth's floor.

By now, Jessica had not only forgotten her argument with her roommate, she'd also convinced herself that the Thetas' request was really no big deal. So Elizabeth had to go out with Peter Wilbourne, so what? There wasn't a woman in the world who didn't go out with a complete creep now and then. It was the hazard of dating. You could never be sure that the guy who seemed okay when he asked you to the movies wouldn't turn out to be some loser who snored in the middle of the film or who spent the night talking about megabytes and binary-object files.

Jessica had had dozens of dates with guys just as bad as Peter Wilbourne III. She'd thought at the time the dates would never end, that she'd never survive, but when she looked back on them, they actually made her laugh. Elizabeth would go out with Peter for a few gruesome hours, and later she would laugh about it. "Remember the time I went out with that noxious waste, Peter Wilbourne?" she'd say. "Remember when I had to publicly apologize for telling the world what a septic tank he was? Wasn't that the funniest thing?"

Jessica didn't bother to knock.

Elizabeth was sitting at her desk, concentrating on something she was writing. She looked up as Jessica floated in, pulling off her headset and letting a fizzle of music into the room.

"I knew I'd find my beautiful twin here, working away like a slave on this beautiful autumn day," Jessica said.

Elizabeth looked from Jessica to the window

and back again. "It's raining, Jess," she said. "It may be beautiful out if you're a walrus, but for most of us humans a heavy downpour is less than ideal."

"Oh, come on, Liz." Jessica dropped her wet jacket on Elizabeth's bed and sat on the edge of her desk. "Didn't some poet say something about beauty depending on who's seeing it?" she asked.

Elizabeth smiled. "Something like that."

"Well?" Jessica raised her arms expansively. "When I look outside, I see a beautiful day!"

"I'm glad to hear that, Jess, but I wish you'd sit somewhere else." Elizabeth gave her a little shove. "You're wrinkling my notes."

"Oh, pardon me! I wouldn't want to be responsible for wrinkling your notes." Jessica slid to the floor, dragging several pages covered with Elizabeth's handwriting with her. She reached down to retrieve them. "Don't you ever get tired of doing work all the time?" she asked, not even bothering to glance at them as she put them back on the desk.

Elizabeth gave her an exasperated look. "It's an assignment for the station."

Jessica grinned. "Trying to get in good with the aloof but sexy Tom Watts?" she teased.

"Don't be ridiculous," Elizabeth said, turning away as she straightened out the papers on her desk. "I'm not interested in Tom Watts."

"I'm glad," Jessica said. "Isabella's got a thing

for Tom I'm-Not-Interested-in-Women Watts. I don't think I could stand having the two of you mooning over him."

Elizabeth dropped her pen on the floor. "Well, you don't have to worry about me," she said, her face to the carpet. "It just so happens that I'm not interested in men at the moment, and certainly not in Tom."

"Does that mean you don't have a date for the Homecoming game?" Jessica asked, leaning on the back of her sister's chair.

Elizabeth started writing again. "I'm not going to the game. I want to work on this as much as I can."

"I think you may be wrong about that," Jessica said, using her little-sister voice.

Elizabeth didn't look up. "Forget it, Jess. I don't care if you got yourself two dates for the game and you need me to take one of them—I'm not doing it. I'm staying here and working."

"But Liz . . ." Jessica crouched beside her sister's chair. "It's not that, it's much more important than that. My whole social life at SVU is on the line here."

Elizabeth stopped mid-word and looked at her. Jessica hated it when her sister stared at her like that, as if she could read her thoughts and didn't like what she saw. "This doesn't have something to do with the Thetas, does it?"

How did Elizabeth know things like that? Jessica forced herself to smile. "They just want you to do one little thing to prove your loyalty."

"What little thing?" Elizabeth asked, not returning her smile.

"They just want you to go to the game with Peter Wilbourne," Jessica said in a rush. She was convinced that if she got it out fast enough, Elizabeth wouldn't object as much. "And apologize for reaming him out in public that time."

Elizabeth was looking at her as though she were sprouting fur and fangs.

"They what?"

"They want you—"

"Jessica Wakefield, have you lost your mind completely?" Elizabeth stood up so quickly that Jessica fell over. "Have you been inhaling too many car fumes from the back of Mike McAllery's bike or something? You can't seriously think that I'd go out with Peter Wilbourne!"

"Think of it this way, Liz," Jessica said reasonably, getting to her feet. "You haven't had one date since you've been here. Even though you don't like Peter Wilbourne, it can't hurt your reputation to be seen with the president of the Sigmas."

Elizabeth stared at her. "You are crazy," she said slowly. "You are out of your tiny mind."

"Oh, come on, Liz. It's only one date. A football game doesn't last that long, *and* it's all outdoors. All you have to do is sit there and watch the game and drink a soda and that's it. You don't

even have to talk to him, except to apologize—
which won't take a second. What could be sim-
pler?"

Elizabeth shook her head. "Unbelievable. After
the way that moron treated you and Danny . . . I
just can't believe, I cannot believe you'd even sug-
gest this."

"Liz, the Thetas will change their minds about
pledging me if they change their minds about
pledging you, and they'll definitely change their
minds about you if you don't do this one little
thing."

"I won't do it, Jessica."

Jessica started to wheedle. "Liz, be reasonable.
This isn't the end of the world, you know. It's one
lousy little date. You've been on bad dates before.
You'll laugh about this later, Liz. I guarantee it.
Years from now, all I'll have to say is 'Peter Wil-
bourne' and you'll go into hysterics."

But Elizabeth was way beyond wheedling.

"The only reason I've gone this far with the
Thetas is because of you," she said calmly. "But
this is where I stop. It's bad enough being on the
same planet with scum like Peter Wilbourne; there
is *no way* I'm going to date him. And there is absolutely no way in the universe that I would *apologize* to him."

So what'd you think? Tom was asking himself as
he dribbled the ball past Danny. *Just because she*

156

looked at you like maybe you weren't just another re-
porter, like maybe you were a nice guy, did you think
that meant she was interested? Did you think that be-
cause she was working so hard on the article, it meant
that you'd been wrong about her still being in love
with Wilkins? Did you really think she didn't care if
he got in trouble? Are you an idiot, or what? Tom
raised his arms, aimed, jumped—and watched the
ball bounce off the rim.

"Nice one, Tombo!" Danny shouted, scooping
the ball in one deft motion and slipping around
him. "You should've told me you were on my
team!"

Tom raced after Danny.

I'm an idiot, that's what I am. A complete stooge.
How could I have even thought that I might have a
chance with Elizabeth? She probably wasn't even
thinking about me when she was looking at me like
that. She was probably thinking of him. *It's obvious*
she still worships the guy. She would have thrown that
story back in my face if she'd thought for one second
that he might get hurt by it.

Danny raised the ball, he aimed, he jumped.
Tom jumped too, trying to block the shot.

"Eleven–nothing!" Danny yelled as the ball
dropped through the net. "Nothing, Tombo. As in
none, zero, zilch, *nada.* Nothing to eleven. You
want to quit while I'm ahead?"

And even if there was no Todd Wilkins, and even
if her interest in you wasn't just professional, so then

what? You're going to walk right into it, Tom? You're going to set yourself up to lose something else? If you don't have anything, you don't have anything to lose.

The ball bounced off Tom's head and fell to the ground.

"Hey, Spaceman Watts, I'm talking to you. You want keep going, or you want to quit?"

"I don't know," Tom said, still thinking about Elizabeth. "I just don't know."

Chapter Eight

"What do you mean, you have to go home?"

It took every bit of willpower Jessica possessed to disentangle herself from Mike's arms, but she managed to pull herself up to a sitting position.

"I just noticed the time," she said, pointing to the luminous numbers on the VCR. "I told you, I have to study tonight. I have to get back."

"Oh, baby . . ." He pulled her back down on the couch. "You don't really have to leave me. Stay here and I'll help you study."

"Oh, sure you will," Jessica said with a smile. "But this isn't biology, it's English."

"'Parting is such sweet sorrow . . .'" Mike whispered, his lips against her ear. "That's Shakespeare. You can't get any more English than that."

Jessica could feel her heart weakening. Maybe she didn't have to study *that* much. Tomorrow's exam wasn't the final or anything like that. It was just an exam. And they were allowed to refer to the text. How hard could it be when you had your book open in front of you?

But then a voice that wasn't Mike's started whispering in her ear. *You haven't finished one assignment, passed one test, or gone to more than two classes in a day since you started seeing Mike,* this voice was saying. *Never mind about what a sweet sorrow parting is. If you flunk out of college, your parents will have you back home before you and Mike have a chance to say good-bye.*

"No, Mike," Jessica said, once more struggling to a sitting position. "I really have to go. I've got to start paying more attention to my schoolwork or—"

Mike groaned. "I don't believe this. Isn't it bad enough I have to be jealous of every guy with eyes in Southern California—now I have to be jealous of some old textbook, too?"

She leaned into the hands that were caressing her. She could feel her body giving up the fight. Her body didn't want to go back to a dorm room and sit at a desk; her body wanted to stay here with these warm hands stroking it and that soft mouth on hers.

You have enough trouble with your brother, that unpleasant, whiny voice said. *If he finds out you're doing badly in school, he'll make sure you stop seeing Mike, don't think he won't.*

Jessica tore herself away from those hands. "Mike, please," she pleaded. "You know I'd rather stay here with you than go back to the dorm, but I have to get some work done or I'll get kicked out of school."

He ran his fingers tenderly down the side of her face. "Well, I've been thinking about this very thing, and I have the solution to the problem," he said softly. "I know how you can be with me *and* concentrate on school at the same time."

Jessica smiled. She had enough trouble concentrating on things like eating and sleeping when she was with Mike. "Oh, really? And what would that be?"

"Live here."

She couldn't have heard him right.

"What?"

"Live here." He looked as though this were the most normal, obvious proposal in the world. "Move in with me. Then you don't ever have to go home. You'll already be here." He touched his mouth to her hair. "Then I don't have to lie awake at night, thinking about you."

"But Michael—"

She didn't know what to say. She hadn't dared hope that he lay in bed at night thinking about her the way she lay awake thinking about him. She was afraid to ask him what his real feelings for her were.

"But what? It's the answer to everything. You move in, and then we can see each other all we want."

Her heart and her body wanted her to say yes. The idea of always being with him was almost too much happiness to bear. Every cell in her body seemed to be zinging with joy.

But that insistent little voice in her head had its doubts. *Move in with him?* it was shrieking. *You don't just move in with someone after a few weeks! Moving in with someone is a big step. A very big step. Do you have any idea what your parents would do if they found out? They'd kill you. And don't think they wouldn't find out. Steven lives upstairs, Jessica. Are you planning to buy a dark wig and wear sunglasses for the next four years?*

"Come on, baby, what's the problem? Just say yes."

Jessica could feel herself getting lost in those seductive golden eyes. "This is something I'm really going to have to think about, Mike," she said, forcing herself to her feet.

As much as she loved Mike, even Jessica knew that living with someone was different than being in love with them. It meant a real commitment. Commitment had never been one of her strong points.

"What's there to think about?" He stood up too, putting his arms around her. "Who would you rather live with? Me or Isabella?"

You! her heart screamed. *You!*

"It's not that I don't want to, Mike," she answered as the warmth of his lips touched her neck. "It's just that it's a big step. I really need some time to think it over."

"Okay," he whispered. "But don't take too long. You know I hate to be kept waiting."

*　　*　　*

"You know, Steven," Billie said, looking up from the paper she was reading. "I had a brilliant idea this morning for making a little extra money."

"Umph," Steven said. He was sitting on the sofa, staring into space.

"I was thinking we should get some of those outdoor wooden benches they sell at Hechingers, and paint them with flowers and all sorts of wild colors to sell at the flea market on Cantina Boulevard on Saturday for people's lawns."

"Umph," Steven said. He frowned in concentration, listening for something.

"It's the kind of thing people who shop at that flea market will love," Billie continued. "Don't you think?"

"Umph."

"How many do you think we could sell?"

"Umph."

Billie threw her paper onto the coffee table. "Steven Wakefield, have you heard one word I said?"

Steven didn't hear her. A motorcycle engine had started up outside and he was listening to that.

Billie sighed in frustration. "That's not Mike," she said as Steven jumped to his feet and went running to the window. "That's a BMW. He's got a Kawasaki engine."

Steven turned to look at her as the BMW pulled into the street. "How did you know that?"

"How did I know what?" Billie asked. "How

did I know Mike McAllery's bike has a Kawasaki engine? Or how did I know that was what you were listening for?"

He grinned sheepishly. "Both."

"I know what engine Mike's bike has because he explained it to me one day when I happened to run into him downstairs and asked him if he put the bike together himself." She gave Steven a look. "He did. I know you think he's probably a gunrunner for some guerrilla army, but he happens to be a first-class mechanic." She gave Steven another look. "And I knew that was what you were listening for because living with you is like living with a CIA agent. All you do lately is skulk around trying to catch Mike with Jessica."

The sheepish grin returned. "I know you think I'm crazy, Billie, but I can't help it. The thought of Jessica throwing herself away on a piece of trash like that—"

With another sigh, Billie went over and put her arms around him. "Steven," she said, "I love you. You know that, don't you? But you have got to get a grip on yourself. You know nothing about this man except that you don't like the way he looks—"

Steven stiffened. "That's not true, Billie. I know he's a womanizer. I know he runs around drinking and doing God knows what till all hours of the morning. I know he's always having an argument with someone."

"Steven, you're prelaw. You have also got to

164

know that all your evidence is circumstantial."

"It's not circumstantial, Billie, it's gut instinct."

She took her arms away. "And my gut instinct is making me rethink our whole relationship."

He looked at her in surprise. For the first time all evening he was thinking more about her than Mike McAllery. "What do you mean?"

"I mean that if we ever got married, I'm not so sure we should have children. If this is how you act when your *sister* starts having a serious relationship, how will you act when it's your own daughter?"

Steven laughed. "Oh, come on, Billie. That's ridiculous. That—"

He broke off as a sound from the street caught his attention. "Don't tell me *that's* not the motorcycle from hell," he said, sticking his head out the window. He made a fist. "It is!" he hissed. "He's taking her home."

Billie put a hand on his shoulder. "Well, that should make you happy. It isn't even nine o'clock and he's taking her home. She isn't spending the night."

"Why should that make me happy?" he asked, turning to face her. "He's probably just getting rid of Jess so he can have another date."

Lila Fowler—or the Contessa di Mondicci, as she was now known—appeared in Jessica's dream. She was wearing a tailored gray dress and matching coat and hat. She had a diamond as big as a Ping-

Pong ball on her left hand. The count was with her. He wore a dark business suit and had a distracted air. He talked on a cellular phone the whole time. The Contessa di Mondicci was bored.

"It's not that I don't love Tisiano to death," she told Jessica, "but he is *so* busy . . . and there are all these formal dinners and functions to go to." She shrugged, her wedding ring flashing like a strobe light. "Still, I can't complain. When I think of you, Jessica, living in a dorm with a bunch of *girls* . . . You can't really experience what it's like to be a woman until you live with a man."

Jessica was wearing a chartreuse cat suit and Mike's old motorcycle jacket. Her hair was blowing in the wind. She laughed. "Live in a dorm?" Jessica said. "But I don't live in a dorm."

"You don't?" Lila asked.

Jessica shook her head. "Of course not. And I know exactly what it's like to be a woman," she said as Mike pulled up behind her on his bike. "I live with *him*," she said, slipping into his arms and a passionate kiss. When finally they broke apart, Jessica turned back to the Contessa di Mondicci. "And believe me," she said, "I'm not bored . . ."

Jessica woke up, her lips still tingling with Mike's kiss. She'd been wrong to leave last night. And maybe she was wrong to hesitate about moving in with him too. All she could think of was seeing him again.

Frantic with love, Jessica looked at the clock. If she hurried, she could surprise him with his favorite breakfast, lemon croissants and blueberry jam, before her first class.

Jessica flung herself out of bed and started rummaging through the pile of clothes on her desk for something to wear.

Isabella rolled over, slowly opening her eyes. "Where are you going?" she asked sleepily. "The alarm hasn't even gone off yet."

"I'm hungry," Jessica said, her hand on the doorknob. "I'm going to get something to eat."

Jessica floated all the way to Mike's. *I've been a fool,* she told herself. *Of course I should move in with him. That's what you do when you love someone as much as I love him. You want to be with them as much as you can. You want to share everything with them, from breakfast to brushing your teeth at night.*

She hugged the warm croissants to her body as she raced along. How would Mike react when he opened his door and found her standing there; when she told him that she'd brought him the first of the thousands of breakfasts they were going to share? Would he be surprised? Would he pretend he'd known she'd give in? Or would he just be so overcome with joy that he'd take her into his arms without saying a word?

Jessica practically ran across the street to Mike's building and up the stairs. She was so excited, so nervous about actually telling him her decision, that she'd gone past his floor and was almost at her brother's landing before she realized her mistake.

Relax a little, she told herself. *Catch your breath. Walk, don't run. You're a woman now. Don't act like a teenager.*

Halfway back down the stairs to Mike's floor, she stopped suddenly.

"I want to thank you," a male voice was saying. A male voice that was imprinted on her soul. "That was terrific. It really was."

What was he doing up so early? What was he doing out in the hall? Maybe he'd had some emergency with the plumbing and he'd had to get the janitor out of bed to fix it. Sure, that was what had happened. He was talking to the janitor.

Jessica was just about to call out to him when another voice spoke. It was not the voice of the janitor. It was a female voice. A revoltingly sweet and cloying female voice.

"Don't mention it," it said. "You know you can call me anytime."

Jessica felt the stairs disappear out from under her. It was all she could do not to collapse. Horrified, she watched a very pretty redhead hurry down the stairs, smiling to herself. She heard Mike turn and go back to his apartment. She dropped the bag of croissants and followed the other girl down the stairs. Only Jessica wasn't smiling to herself. Jessica was sobbing.

"I'm not going to the Homecoming dance either," Nina said as she and Elizabeth made their way through the breakfast line. "I have a big paper due for my history of science course." She put a glass of juice on her tray and gave Elizabeth a look. "What's your excuse?"

Elizabeth, counting calories in her head to determine whether she should have granola or oatmeal, frowned. "I don't need an excuse," she said. "No one's asked me."

Nina handed her a container of skim milk. "You know, I'm really, really sorry that I encouraged you to go see Todd that morning. I guess I should have warned you that I'm good when it comes to theoretical physics and advanced calculus, but not very good when it comes to men."

"Neither am I, anymore," Elizabeth said with a laugh. She picked up her tray and followed Nina into the dining hall. "And anyway, it's not your fault I got my signals crossed with Todd. I think I've finally come to terms with the fact that it really is over between us."

Nina led the way to a table in a corner. "It's really been hard for you, hasn't it?" she asked.

Elizabeth took a deep breath. "It's been easier losing the three quarters of a pound I've lost by living on air and water for the last few weeks than it has been getting used to the fact that Todd isn't part of my life anymore." She plunked down across from Nina and started to eat, her mind still on Todd. It was strange, but even though she knew in her heart that it wouldn't have worked between her and Todd, she still missed him.

"I guess it'll just take longer than I thought," she added with a bleak smile. "Doesn't everybody say that time heals all wounds?"

Nina laughed. "I always thought it was time wounds all heels," she said. "I find that very comforting."

Elizabeth laughed too. "You're right; I feel better already."

Nina nibbled thoughtfully on an English muffin. "You know what else they say, though, don't you?" she asked, eyeing her cautiously.

"Wait a minute, Nina," Elizabeth said, holding up her hands. "Remember what you just said. You're no good when it comes to men."

"But this isn't me," Nina protested. "This is tried and true. I'm sure I read it in one of those women's magazines that are always lying around the TV room."

Elizabeth sighed in mock resignation. "All right," she said, unable to keep herself from smiling. "What else does everybody say?"

The beads on Nina's braids clicked as she gleefully shook her head. "That the quickest way to get over one man is another man."

Elizabeth gazed back at her skeptically. "Really?"

"Uh huh. That's what they say." Nina crossed her heart. "It's tried and true. Handed down from one generation of women to another with recipes for chocolate-chip cookies."

The skeptical look remained on Elizabeth's face. "I don't suppose you have any idea of who this other man might possibly be?" she teased.

Nina pretended to be thinking this over. "Well, there is the guy who always watches you in the library," she said at last.

Unbidden, Elizabeth's heart jumped half a beat. "You mean Tom? Tom Watts?"

Nina shook her head. "No, not Tom. The other one. The one you told me gave you the rose that Celine destroyed."

"William," Elizabeth said. "William White." She seemed to be considering William, but in reality she was thinking about the one who hadn't given her the rose.

"And don't forget, Elizabeth," Nina said, digging into her cereal. "You don't have to wait for him to ask you out. This is the nineties. You can ask him."

"Jessica. Jessica." Isabella sat down at the edge of Jessica's bed and put a tentative hand on her shoulder. "Jessica, why don't you come into the living room and I'll make some coffee and we can talk. You can tell me what happened."

Jessica pushed her hand away.

Isabella put it back. "Jessica, you can't lie here crying all afternoon—you're beginning to scare me." Which was true. Ever since she got back from her last class over half an hour ago, Isabella had been trying

171

unsuccessfully to get her roommate to talk to her.

Jessica raised her tearstained face from her pillow. Her skin was pale and blotchy and her eyes were swollen and red. "Yes, I can," she said in a hoarse, choked voice. "I'm going to lie here crying for the rest of my life."

"You can't," Isabella said. "The rate you're going, you'll be dried up by dinner."

"I don't care!" Jessica wailed, throwing herself back down on the bed. "I don't care what happens to me anymore. I don't care if I shrivel up and blow away."

Isabella gave her a shake. "Come on, Jess," she coaxed. "I'll make some coffee, and we'll sit on the couch and you can tell me exactly what happened. You'll feel better once you've talked about it."

"No, I won't," came the muffled reply. "I'll never feel better again."

The first time Elizabeth reached the door of the TV station, she kept right on walking.

"I can't do it," she mumbled to herself as she hurried by. "I just can't do it."

Ever since she and Tom had gone over her notes together, she hadn't been able to stop thinking about him. She couldn't figure him out. Sometimes she could sense a bond between them so strong that it almost frightened her, and other times he was so cold and distant that she was convinced he didn't like her at all.

It was crazy, but there had been a moment that afternoon when she almost felt as if he might kiss her. And then he'd brought up Todd, and an invisible wall had sprung up between them. She couldn't decide whether Tom thought she was helping him because she wanted to get back at Todd, or if he thought she would throw the story away if it did turn out that Todd was implicated in some way.

Elizabeth came to the end of the path. Maybe she should just keep going. She had an interview with Manny Clipper, the basketball coach, in half an hour. She might as well go a little early and use the time to see what she could pick up in the athletics office.

"That's what I'll do," Elizabeth announced to no one. "I'll go ahead to my interview."

Instead, she turned around and went back the way she'd just come.

Although she couldn't tell whether or not Tom liked her, Elizabeth was beginning to realize how she felt about him. She was terrified of starting a new relationship on the rebound from Todd, but in spite of this it was getting harder and harder to kid herself about Tom any longer. She felt enormously attracted to him. She had from the first moment she saw him. Not because of his unusual good looks, but because of his character and strength. Tom Watts wasn't fooled by appearances, and he didn't let anyone push him around.

Once more, Elizabeth found herself standing in

front of the door to the television station. She stared at the sign on the door as though she'd never seen it before. WSVU it said in bold black letters, and underneath in smaller print, *Studio and Office*.

It's not going to work, Elizabeth decided. *I just can't do it, and that's that.*

She spun on her heel and headed back in the other direction. Whether Tom liked her or didn't like her, whether she was interested in him because she was on the rebound from Todd or not, it didn't matter. She was never going to be able to ask him to the Homecoming ball, and that was all there was to it. Everyone knew that Tom Watts was a loner. He wasn't interested in women or having a relationship; he was interested only in the news.

I must be insane, Elizabeth told herself as she reached the end of the path once more, turned around, and marched back toward the station. *I must really be crazy. Of course he isn't interested in me. I'm just a reporter to him. That's all he cares about. That's all I'll ever be.*

She stopped in front of the door once again. She put her hand out toward the knob. She touched it. She pulled away and turned around so fast that she slammed into someone coming up behind her.

"Oh, I'm sorry!" Elizabeth gasped. "I'm really sorry."

She could feel herself blushing as she looked into his face, but his hands were on her shoulders, steadying her, and in that instant she knew she could do it. She could ask him to the dance. "Tom, I—"

He dropped his hands suddenly. "Wait a minute. What are you doing here?" Tom demanded. "You're supposed to be interviewing Coach Clipper this afternoon. You're going to be late."

"Me? I—"

"You're not changing your mind about this, are you? You aren't having second thoughts?"

He wasn't even looking at her. He was riffling around in his stupid notebook. "Because if you are—"

It was true. Why didn't she just face it? It was only about work. It would only ever be about work. "No!" Elizabeth said, resisting the urge to kick him in the shins. "I'm not changing my mind about *that*."

Jessica had been afraid that if she told Isabella about seeing the redhead coming out of Mike's apartment, Isabella would say the dreaded I-told-you-so. *What did you expect?* she'd imagined Isabella saying. *Didn't I try to warn you? Didn't I tell you what he's like?* She'd even been afraid that Isabella might know who the other girl was. *Tall and striking with legs to her earlobes? Oh, I know who she is. She and Mike go back a long way!*

But Isabella said none of those things. Instead, she made coffee, opened the chocolate macaroons she'd been saving for a special occasion, and listened silently while Jessica poured out her tale of woe.

"You poor thing," she said when Jessica was finished. There wasn't a trace of sarcasm in her voice or on her face. "How totally awful. No wonder you're so upset."

Jessica dried her eyes with one of the tissues from the box Isabella had put beside her.

"I just couldn't believe it, Isabella," Jessica said, her voice still thick with emotion. "After all that's happened between us . . ." *After making love to me, and calling me his baby, and begging me to live with him* . . . "It was like being knifed in the heart."

"I'm sure it was," Isabella said gently. "Believe me, Jess, I've been there once or twice myself, and I know exactly what you're going through." She sipped her coffee. "It's better you didn't confront him there and then," Isabella continued. "You know what men are like. He'd probably have a dozen excuses. She was his cousin, or his cleaning lady, or an old friend he owed money to." Isabella made a comical face. "You wouldn't believe the stories they come up with."

Feeling a little better just to have told someone, Jessica broke a cookie in half. Maybe she should have confronted Mike right then. She'd love to hear how he'd explain the redhead.

And then a thought occurred to Jessica that hadn't occurred to her before. What if he *could* explain her?

176

Isabella started telling her some of the excuses she'd heard men make, but Jessica wasn't really listening. She was thinking. Did it make any sense that a man would want you and need you one minute, and go off with someone else the next? Did it make any sense that a man would plead with you to live with him and then spend the night with somebody else? No, it didn't. It didn't make any sense at all. There had to be some other reason for the redhead. Obviously she wasn't his cleaning lady—cleaning ladies didn't wear Lycra shorts and tank tops. And she wasn't the janitor. The janitor in Steven's building was sixty and smoked cigars. On the other hand, the janitor might be sick and she might have been helping him out.

"So what are you going to do now?" Isabella asked. "You want me to drop off a Dear-Mike letter for you?"

Jessica looked up in surprise. "What?"

Isabella looked back at her with concern. "What are you going to *do*, Jess? If you don't want to talk to him, the best thing to do might be to write."

Jessica took another macaroon. "I don't know, Isabella. I don't want to be too rash."

"You what?"

She shrugged. "I mean, maybe it wasn't exactly the way it seemed. Maybe I overreacted a little."

"Overreacted?" Isabella repeated.

Jessica nodded. "And besides, I always fought for what was mine in the past. And now Mike

177

McAllery is mine. I can't give him up without a fight, can I?"

Isabella swallowed the rest of her coffee in one gulp. "If you say so."

"It's a good thing I don't have a gun," said Tom to his unopened container of juice. "I'd probably wind up shooting myself." He pushed his half-eaten sandwich away and put his head on his desk with a groan.

What was wrong with him, anyway? It was as if his emotions were a string and he was the yo-yo. One minute he wanted to take Elizabeth into his arms, and the next he was pushing her away.

Tom closed his eyes. He couldn't believe it when she fell into him this afternoon. He couldn't believe how small and fragile she felt in his hands. And she'd looked so lovely. Flushed, bright-eyed, and out of breath; he couldn't remember ever seeing her look more beautiful. She looked the way she had in his dream. Expectant, excited, happy to see him.

Had she been happy to see him? He didn't know anymore. He'd been so surprised to see her—as though she'd materialized out of his thoughts—and so rattled, that he couldn't get rid of her fast enough. Seeing her there when she should have been on her way to the athletics office, he'd been sure she was going to back out of the story. She'd looked so confused and so nervous that he knew she was going to tell him she couldn't go on. She'd been thinking it over, and she couldn't risk hurting Todd. Not even when truth and fairness were at stake.

And that was why he'd yelled at her. He could still see the look on her face. She looked as though he'd slapped her.

"Tom?"

This is all I need, Tom thought. *Now I'm hearing her voice when I'm alone.*

"Tom?"

Not only was he hearing her voice, but her voice was upset and needed him.

"Tom, I'm really sorry to bother you, but . . ."

He raised his head and turned around.

She was standing in the doorway, strained and pale, her notebook clutched in her hand. It was hard to tell because half of the lights were off, but she looked as though she were close to tears.

"What is it, Elizabeth?" He got to his feet.

Slowly, as though this were a dream, she came toward him, holding out the book.

He took it from her. "Todd?" he asked.

She nodded. "You were right," she whispered. "He is implicated."

And he'd also been right that she was close to tears. "You want to forget about this?" he asked, chucking truth and justice out the window. "We can jack it, Elizabeth. Do something else."

But she was shaking her head. "All I want is to believe it isn't true."

Chapter Nine

Michael McAllery whistled an old rock song under his breath as he strode briskly through the night. He had his hands in his pockets and his collar up against the autumnal chill, and he walked with the air of a man who knew exactly where he was going and why. Halfway down the block he stopped to look in the window of the bookstore; at the corner he played with his keys while he waited for the light to change.

Yet all the while he was unaware that just a few yards behind, a dark figure followed his every step: speeding up when he sped up; stopping when he stopped; ducking into the shadows whenever he turned.

Jessica pulled the scarf more tightly around her face. *Maybe Isabella's right,* she thought as she warily rounded the corner after Mike. *Maybe I really am crazy. Maybe sex hormones have destroyed my brain.*

The idea of trailing Mike had come to her on the spur of the moment. Unable to eat, to concentrate on anything that wasn't him for more than three seconds, or even to cry anymore, Jessica had gone to his apartment to have it out. "Maybe you shouldn't surprise him again," Isabella had advised. "Maybe you should call first." But by then Jessica had convinced herself that he'd be sitting at home wondering why he hadn't heard from her, waiting for her to come by.

He was just leaving the building when she arrived. She'd been about to say something, but she stopped. Suddenly she knew that if she wanted to find out the truth, she needed to be with him when he didn't know she was there. He was probably just going around the corner to pick up some milk—but maybe he wasn't. Maybe he was going to pick up the redhead.

Mike slowed down. Jessica stopped in front of an appliance store, pretending to be mesmerized by the display of toasters and coffee makers while she watched him out of the corner of her eye. He came to a halt under a pink neon sign that said *Mojo's Bar and Grill*, pulled open the door, and disappeared inside.

Jessica's heart was stampeding and her whole body felt damp with sweat. *Stop it*, she told her heart. *Get a grip on yourself. Stop making so much noise.* She wiped her hands on her skirt, the one Mike had said was his favorite because it was the same color as her eyes. *Just give him some time to sit down and get a drink . . . then you can go in and see who he's with.*

Jessica stared at the gleaming appliances in their bright designer colors and shining chrome, but all she could see was fiery red hair.

She started slowly down the street toward the bar. It was impossible to see in. Lighted beer signs and a checkered café curtain filled the smoked-glass window, and even though it was a weeknight the place was packed. Jessica stepped into the doorway of the next place over as a group of men came out of Mojo's.

Mojo's wasn't a sophisticated club or café where a guy like Mike would bring a date. It was a neighborhood bar where a guy like Mike would go to have a drink and forget his troubles when he hadn't heard from his girlfriend all day.

Jessica closed her eyes. "Okay," she whispered out loud. "This is it. On the count of three. One . . . two . . . three . . ."

It took her a few minutes to find him. He was in the back room, playing pool with a lanky man with a long ponytail and a lopsided grin. Jessica got herself a soda from the bar and slid into a dark corner booth where she could watch Mike without his seeing her. Not that there was much chance of that. He was so intent on his game and the beer he was drinking that she probably could have come in wearing bells and flashing lights and he wouldn't have noticed her.

Safe in her corner, Jessica began to relax. She'd been right to follow him. Isabella was wrong. Mike wasn't the slimy two-timing creep she'd warned Jessica about. He wasn't sneaking around with other women. He was just a guy hanging out with his friends, shooting a little pool.

She smiled to herself as he systematically cleared the table while his friend watched in horror. The last ball vanished down the left-hand side pocket, and Mike looked up. His friend smiled and shook his hand. A few of the onlookers whooped and cheered. Jessica was so excited that she jumped to her feet. She was going to go over and congratulate him. She was going to throw her arms around him and give him a big, public kiss.

Jessica was only a few feet from the pool table when she realized that another woman had had the exact same idea. Only the other woman was quicker. She was already in Mike's arms.

Jessica shouted. It wasn't really words, it was just a wail of rage. Everyone in the back room turned to look at her, including Mike and the woman whose arms were around his neck.

"Who's the little tiger?" the woman asked, not moving her head from its position on his chest.

Mike smiled at Jessica. "Shelley's right, you do look like a tiger. What's the matter?"

Finally words came. "You two-timing creep! You lying jerk!"

183

"Looks like you've got yourself a real jealous one this time," Shelley said through her giggles.

Mike started laughing. "Oh, come on, Jess, you've got to be kidding."

But Jessica didn't answer him. She was already running from the bar.

Elizabeth sat at her study carrel, her eyes on the textbook in front of her, her notebook opened to a clean page and her pen in her hand ready to write, but her mind was a million miles away. Her mind was on Todd.

She'd been so sure that Todd couldn't be implicated in any scandal that she'd steamed ahead with the investigation without even thinking. Tom had only been trying to make her take a realistic look at what the outcome might be when he'd suggested that Todd could be involved, but she'd taken his remark as a personal insult. Elizabeth grimaced. How ironic that she, who had known Todd so well and for so long, should have been wrong, and Tom Watts, who probably had never even said hello to Todd, had been right.

Not that being right had made Tom generous or sympathetic. "I told you this might happen," he'd said. "I thought you understood that the truth can hurt." Elizabeth dropped her pen and laid her head on the desk. Maybe she wasn't cut out to be an investigative journalist after all. Maybe she should consider writing articles on food and fashion instead. How much trouble could she cause researching pasta recipes?

Elizabeth groaned inwardly. It was all Alexandra Rollins's fault. While Elizabeth was interviewing Coach Clipper, a few chance remarks Alex had made had come into her head. Something about Mark being lucky he didn't have to study much since his time wasn't taken up only with practice but with people wanting to give dinners for the players all the time. *The way athletes are treated on this campus, you'd think the place was designed for them,* Alex had said. She'd mentioned Mark's new Explorer and going to the spectacularly overpriced Da Vinci's for dinner. Sensing that she might really be on to something, Elizabeth had decided to drop her slightly probing, professional style with Coach Clipper and adopted an attitude of open admiration instead. Hiding behind her California good looks and the sweet, girlish smile that always worked so well for Jessica, Elizabeth had stopped asking for information and started wheedling it out of him.

Gently and innocently, Elizabeth had pumped Coach Clipper about the way the basketball team was treated. Coach Clipper had chatted unguardedly, thinking he was impressing her.

Hoping to open him up even more, Elizabeth had mentioned Todd. "My boyfriend, Todd Wilkins," she'd said, praying that Coach Clipper wouldn't know that she'd left out the tiny word *ex*.

He hadn't known. At the mention of Todd, the

coach became almost effusive. "One of the best players we've got," he'd boasted. "And believe me, it cost us the sun and moon to get him. But I'm sure I don't have to tell you how many top-notch universities were after him."

He hadn't had to tell her. Elizabeth had fought back a sour smile. She'd believed that Todd picked SVU and not one of the bigger schools because of her. Apparently she'd been wrong about that, too.

Elizabeth groaned out loud. She wished she'd never started this. She wished it were last week and Tom was showing her the stuff he'd uncovered, and instead of saying that she thought it looked like the biggest story she'd ever touched she'd said, "It's not one for me, Tom. Get somebody else."

"Elizabeth? I was hoping I'd find you here."

She didn't move. If she didn't move he might just go away. It wasn't all just Alexandra Rollins's fault, it was his fault too.

He came around the desk and knelt down beside her chair. "Elizabeth," he whispered. "I've gone over your notes again, and I've been giving this a lot of thought . . ."

She raised her head, brushing a few stray tears from her eyes. "And?"

"Here." Tom reached in his pocket and handed her a tissue. "And I've decided that we don't have to take this any further. I mean, what's the point? There's no question that the sports teams are really important to the school. Whatever's gone on that hasn't been completely aboveboard was to help SVU, not hurt it. It's not like these things have been done for any personal gain."

"What about truth and justice?" she whispered back, hardly able to speak. "What about fairness and honesty?"

Tom handed her another tissue. "Everybody has to compromise sometime, Elizabeth. Nothing's black and white. The trick is knowing when to compromise and when to push."

Elizabeth stared at Tom, torn between gratitude for the generosity of his gesture and disgust that her own weakness should have forced him to make such a sacrifice. Suddenly everything fell into place. The scandal and the shock and hurt it would cause when it broke wasn't Alexandra's fault, or Tom's fault, or even her fault. It was the fault of people who believed that the ends justified the means.

She took the tissue he was offering her and blew her nose. "In that case," she said, "I think this is the time to push."

"Is Elizabeth still working at the station with Tom Watts?" William asked.

Celine looked up from shaking ketchup on her fries. Ever since she'd told William that Tom was training Elizabeth, he didn't let a day go by without asking about it. She wouldn't have thought that someone like William would even be aware of

Tom's existence, but he was more than aware. He was disturbed.

"Working with him?" Celine smiled. "I'd say that those two might be doing a little bit more than working." She picked up a fry and bit off the end. "If you know what I mean."

William eyed her coldly over the rim of his coffee cup. "No, Celine, I don't know what you mean. Are you saying that Elizabeth's going out with Tom?"

"Oh, no, William. I didn't mean to imply that," Celine protested, even though that was exactly what she'd meant.

Ever since she'd discovered that William White was worried about Tom Watts, she'd been determined to give him something to worry about. It didn't matter to Celine if she had to stretch the truth now and then to do so. It didn't matter if she had to out-and-out lie. Tom Watts was a weak point in William, and she was going to make the most of it. How much Elizabeth actually saw Tom or how close they were wasn't important at all.

She finished her fry and delicately licked the oil from her fingertips. "All I meant was that Elizabeth seems to be spending quite a lot of time with Tom." Celine shrugged. "I guess it's this story they're working on. As far as I can tell, they're together every night."

William sipped his coffee without comment, but the glacier-blue eyes were deep in calculation.

"Frankly, I'm a little surprised," Celine went on. "I wouldn't have thought that Tom Watts was really the princess's type."

The pale eyelashes flickered, but he still didn't speak.

"I mean, he's not really a big man on campus, is he? Not anymore. I suppose some girls would find him attractive in a sort of renegade way, but he isn't what you'd call *classically* good looking, is he?" She bit into another fry. "Or blond," she added, wiping a dab of ketchup from the corner of her mouth.

The classically good-looking and blond William White continued to study her wordlessly.

Celine smiled. "Of course, you never can tell with these sweet, virginal types, can you?" she asked. "You think they're into poetry and moonlight walks and what they really want is some cowboy to pull them onto the back of his horse."

William put his cup into its saucer with a click. "There are times, Celine," he said softly, "when I'd really love some cowboy to pull *you* onto the back of a horse." His lips twitched. "Preferably one that bucks."

Why is my life like this? Winston wondered. *Why can't things be normal for me?*

Winston was sitting at a table in the center of the snack bar, surrounded by five of the most attractive girls on campus. He should have been happy, he knew that. He could tell from the glances other guys gave him when they walked past that he should be happy. His ego should be in overdrive and he should be delirious with joy. But he wasn't. He felt like a piece of cheese waiting for the mouse, or, in this case, mice.

Anoushka's plan was simple. These five women of Oakley Hall, wing B, were going to show signs of giving in to the advances of the Sigmas. They were going to string them along for a few days and encourage them to ask them to the Homecoming ball. And then, at the very last minute, to a woman, they were going to say they already had dates. Total humiliation for the Sigmas and total triumph for the good women of Oakley Hall. Simple but fiendishly clever. Winston sighed. A plan like that could have come only from a female brain.

How did I ever get involved in this? he moaned silently.

"They're here," Anoushka said. "Bill just came through the door."

Winston stared at her. Anoushka and Debbie had their heads together and their faces buried in a math book.

"I don't know if I can go through with this," Debbie whispered. "What if I start laughing?"

"You better not," Denise said. She kicked Candy under the table. Winston knew she had because he was sitting next to Denise and her leg brushed against his. Electric sparks went off in his kneecap.

Candy studied her nails. "They see us," she hissed. "They're nudging each other."

"They're headed this way," Maia said.

"I'm out of here," Winston announced. He started to get to his feet.

Denise grabbed his belt and yanked him back down. "Not so fast, Winnie. You can't go yet. If you leave, they won't come over."

Part of Winston didn't want Denise ever to let go of his belt, but another part felt the instinct of a fox who will gnaw off his own foot to get out of a trap.

"Sure they will—" he began.

A booming, boyish voice cut him off.

"Win, old man. How's it going?"

Winston looked up, but the girls continued to pretend that they were so involved in their books they hadn't noticed the gaggle of Sigmas looming over their table.

"Hey, Bill!" Winston could only hope that he looked surprised and not just scared out of his wits. "Jeff, Bruce, Tony, Miles . . ." He nodded to Bill's companions. "I think you've already met my dorm-mates . . ."

"Mind if we join you?" Bruce asked, already shoving a chair between Winston and Denise.

Jeff leaned over Debbie's shoulder. "What are you doing?" he asked.

If Winston had asked Debbie that question, she would have snapped back something like, "Picking my toenails, you idiot, what does it look like I'm doing?"

"I'm trying to understand how to construct a statistical graph," she said to Jeff, looking helpless and cute. Winston knew perfectly well she could draw up a statistical graph with her eyes closed and a parade coming through the room.

Jeff pulled up a chair. "Maybe I can help," he said, practically shoving Anoushka out of his way. "I'm pretty good at math."

Miles, meanwhile, was gazing at Candy like a sheep that had been locked out of the pasture for too long. "Can I . . . uh . . . give you a hand with something?" he said, looking around for another empty chair.

"I'm not doing anything," Candy said with a smile as sweet as her name.

"That's okay," Miles said agreeably. "I can help you with that."

Tom leaned back in his chair. After he'd walked Elizabeth to her dorm from the library, he'd returned to the station to do some more work on the sports-recruitment story, but for once working wasn't stopping him from thinking. It was the other way around.

Every time he looked down at his notebook he saw Elizabeth's face, her blue-green eyes rimmed

192

with tears. He was sure she'd made the right decision about going with the piece—and he was sure she was sure that she'd made the right decision too—but being right didn't always make you feel very good.

And as for being right, had he done the right thing, going after her like that? Tom wished he knew. His first attempts to comfort her had been so inadequate that he'd had to do something to try to make it up to her. *I thought you understood that the truth can hurt.* Tom groaned. What had made him say a cliché like that? *And I told you so.* He'd actually said *I told you so.* But his second attempts to comfort her hadn't been much better.

What he'd wanted to do was simply take her in his arms and whisper clichés into her ear till the library closed—till the universe closed, if it came to that. *Everything's going to be all right,* he longed to tell her. *You're not alone. I'll always be there for you. I'll always take care of you. Always . . .*

But, of course, he hadn't said any of those things. She frightened him so much; his feelings for her frightened him so much. . . .

Tom stared at the wall. This time it wasn't Elizabeth's face he was seeing; this time it was the faces of his family—his parents, his older sister, his little brother.

It was harder to picture them now. The time that had passed and the power of what he felt for them blurred the images. He still missed them so much it was like a physical ache.

It's me who's alone, he said to himself. It wasn't that Elizabeth needed him. It was he who needed her. And needing was something he didn't want to touch with the tip of his finger. It was even more terrifying than love.

What was it Danny had said to him the other day? "You can't start a fire, Tombo, without the risk of getting burned. But without a fire, you'll freeze to death."

Jessica parked the Jeep in the municipal lot and set off to meet Isabella for a mini-shopping spree. There was something about spending money that always cheered her up.

And I could definitely use a little cheering up today, she admitted as she turned onto the main street. *I made an absolute fool of myself last night.*

She could see that now. She'd be lucky if Mike ever spoke to her again after the way she behaved. Everyone in the bar must have laughed themselves silly after she stormed out like that.

Jessica shuddered at the thought. In the bright light of this beautiful afternoon it was easy to see that she had overreacted last night. Totally overreacted. After all, it wasn't as though Mike had gone to the bar with that woman. She was a waitress, that was all. Regulars in bars like that always hugged their favorite waitress. It didn't mean anything. It was like hugging your dog. Mike had probably known Shelley for years. He probably saw her two or three times a week. He probably bought little presents for her kids at Christmas.

Jessica stopped at the corner, waiting for the light to change.

On the other side of the street, a striking-looking couple was getting into a vintage convertible Karmann Ghia with a dented left fender and a lot of body rust. The woman was tall and dark, with the angular face and body of a high-fashion model.

The man was Mike.

This time Jessica was too numb to scream. Scream? If she'd had to jump out of the way of a runaway car, she would have been hit. *Three days, three different women!* her heart was shouting. *He probably has a different woman for every day of the week, like underwear!*

Even above the sounds of the street, she could hear the doors of the Karmann Ghia slam shut. She heard the engine start up. And she saw Mike see her as the high-fashion model pulled the car into traffic. But she couldn't see if he was smiling or not, because there were too many tears in her eyes.

"I don't know why you came here," Todd said as he nervously showed her into his room. "I thought we'd said just about everything there is to say."

Elizabeth stood in the center of the carpet, her arms folded in front of her. She wasn't quite sure why she'd come either, but after Tom left her at her dorm she'd decided she had to talk to Todd.

She had to tell him about the story, to warn him. But Todd wasn't making what was already hard any easier.

"Not quite everything, Todd. Something just happened that I really have to—"

"Here," he said, throwing a pile of books and sweaters from the armchair. "Why don't you sit down?" He smiled awkwardly. "Make yourself comfortable."

Comfortable? The only way she could feel comfortable right now was if somebody knocked her unconscious. Elizabeth shook her head. "I'd rather stand, if you don't mind. What I have to say won't take that long."

"How about coffee or a soda? There's a machine just down the hall."

Since when had he become the host of the year? Why wouldn't he just let her talk?

She shook her head again. "No, really, Todd. I just wanted to tell you—"

"Please, Liz," he interrupted. "I can't deal with this if you're going to stand there like that." He sat down on the edge of his bed. "Sit in the chair. Please?"

She sat in the chair. "Todd, I'm here because I wanted to—"

He cut her off again. "There's just no point in going over the same thing again and again," he said. "I still have feelings for you too, Liz, but you've got to get on with your life."

"Todd, this is not about *my* life. This is about *your* life. About—"

His voice rushed over hers. "My life includes Lauren now, Liz. You've got to understand that."

"Todd!" She shot out of the chair. "I don't care about Lauren! That's not why I'm here."

He stood up too. "Don't shout at me, Liz. I know you're upset about what's happened—"

"I have to shout or you won't listen!" she shouted. "Todd, I'm not here to talk about us. I'm here because there are going to be charges of illegal sports recruitment at this college. Charges in which you're implicated."

That shut him up. For one frozen second Todd just stood there looking at her.

"What?"

As succinctly as she could, Elizabeth told him about what she and Tom had uncovered. She explained that she'd agreed to do the story because she'd been so sure that he couldn't be involved. She told him what Coach Clipper had said.

"And you think that's true?" he asked when she was done. "You think that's why I came here? Because they offered me money and privileges?"

I thought you came here because of me. Because you loved me and couldn't stand to be apart. But she couldn't say that out loud, not anymore. Elizabeth stared back in silence, unable to speak.

Todd was shaking his head. "I can't believe you'd think that," he said. "I thought you knew

197

me a lot better than that."

"So did I," Elizabeth whispered.

"I'm sorry, Mike," Isabella said, "but as I've already told you three times, Jessica doesn't want to talk to you." Isabella didn't sound sorry at all.

Jessica kept her face in the cushion of the sofa, forcing herself not to jump up and grab the phone. Of course, *she* knew that Isabella had been right all along. *She* knew that Mike McAllery was nothing but a two-timing creep. *She* knew that the only thing she had to say to him was good-bye. But Jessica's stupid heart hadn't gotten the message yet. Jessica's heart still longed to hear his voice, to hear him call her baby.

"Mike, how can I put this so you'll understand?" Isabella said. "She doesn't want to speak to you."

Jessica sobbed into the couch. She was just going to have to be stronger than her heart. Especially in front of Isabella. Isabella had been comforting her for hours now. Jessica couldn't let her see that she felt anything for Mike except loathing.

Isabella's voice got louder and harder. "No, Mike. Even if you died and came back as someone else, she wouldn't want to speak to you."

Jessica looked up as Isabella slammed down the receiver. She wiped away another flood of tears. "I can't believe I was such a fool," she sniffled. "I just can't believe it . . ." She took another tissue from the box on the coffee table and blew her nose.

"Come on, Jess," Isabella said, setting down two steaming mugs. "Try some of Grandma Ricci's almond espresso. It'll make you feel better."

Fresh tears streamed down Jessica's cheeks. "I'll never feel better again as long as I live. I'll always feel like this. Like somebody's just run over my heart with a tractor."

Isabella sat down beside her on the couch. "No, you won't, Jess. In a little while you'll feel like your heart had a fender bender with a compact car, and then you'll feel like it walked into a wall, and then you'll be looking around for the next guy to mow it down."

"Not me," Jessica croaked. She would never love anyone the way she'd loved Mike. She wouldn't let herself. "I'm never going to be that stupid again. The next guy who asks me out is going to have to produce letters of reference and a ten-year guarantee."

Isabella handed her the coffee. "That's what you say now—"

"No, I mean it. I'm through with men." Jessica turned to Isabella with her old look of determination. "To think that I almost blew the Thetas for that creep. How could I? How could I have jeopardized my chances with them for *him?*"

"Drink the coffee," Isabella said. "Caffeine's wonderful for anger."

"That would have been too much!" Jessica

wailed. "To lose Mike *and* lose the Thetas. Then I'd really know my life was over."

Isabella looked at her uneasily. "This may not be the right time to mention it, Jess," she said hesitantly. "But you're not out of the woods yet."

Jessica looked at her sharply. "What are you—" Suddenly she drew in her breath. Elizabeth! She'd been so upset over Mike that she'd completely forgotten about Elizabeth! Elizabeth refused to go out with Peter Wilbourne. Elizabeth was going to sabotage Jessica's last chance at happiness.

"Oh, my God," Jessica groaned. "I forgot about Liz."

"Well, Alison Quinn hasn't forgotten about her. She was asking me today why Elizabeth hadn't gotten in touch with Peter the Terrible yet."

Jessica put her head in her hands. "What did you say?"

"I said I didn't know. I said I'd ask you." Isabella put a hand on her shoulder. "Maybe if I talk to Alison, Jess. You know, she and I go back a long way. Maybe if I try to explain—"

Jessica's head bobbed up. "Explain what?"

Isabella blinked. "Explain that Elizabeth refuses point-blank to go on the date."

"But she doesn't," Jessica said, a glint of excitement showing through the tears. "Liz is going out with Peter Wilbourne the Third. And she's going to have a great time."

Isabella stared back at her uncomprehendingly

for a few seconds, and then, slowly, understanding dawned. "You mean you're going to pretend to be your sister?"

For the first time since she saw Mike with Miss Karmann Ghia, Jessica allowed herself a small smile. "It's always worked before," she said. "There have been times when I've been Elizabeth better than she could have been herself."

Some guys got so nervous before a big game that they couldn't sleep or eat beforehand. If they did manage to get to sleep, they dreamed that they single-handedly lost the game, and woke up sweating. If they did manage to eat some breakfast, they'd throw it up in the locker room. All these guys had to do was imagine the bleachers filled with spectators and the coach watching from the sidelines, and they'd go to pieces.

But not Tom Watts. In the days when Tom was the biggest collegiate quarterback on the West Coast, he never got nervous before a game. He got excited and keyed up, sure, but not nervous. Not nervous like he was now.

In his jacket pocket was an envelope, and in the envelope was a poem he'd written to Elizabeth. He never could have explained his feelings out loud, but he had put them down in this poem. Not only had he told her exactly how he felt about her, but he'd also explained that there was something in his past that stopped him from taking any chances on love.

Although he'd already wiped his palms on his jeans at least six times since leaving the station, Tom wiped them again as Dickenson Hall came into view.

"I must be crazy," he muttered to himself as he came to a stop under a tree. "I must be at least ten cards short of a full deck."

It would have been crazy enough if he'd simply spent the evening writing an emotionally charged poem to Elizabeth. That in itself would have been grounds for having himself put away in some nice, quiet padded cell. But what was he doing actually *delivering* the poem? Didn't he have any sense left? Any self-respect? One tiny shred of self-preservation? Tom leaned his head against the tree. He couldn't decide if he was on automatic pilot or self-destruct.

This time Tom wiped his hands on the sleeve of his jacket. At least he wasn't so insane that he intended to hand it to her in person. He couldn't bear the thought of being there when she read it. What if she laughed? What if she was so horrified that he should have any feelings for her that she gave up her job at WSVU? No, he was going to slip it into her mailbox and be gone before anyone saw him.

Tom took a deep breath, his eyes on Dickenson Hall. That was, he was going to slip it into her mailbox if he could get himself across the street and through the doors of her dorm.

Just do it, he urged himself. *If you're going to do*

it, then do it. He took another deep breath. No, facing an opposing team of men built like Sherman tanks hadn't scared him at all. But being caught by Elizabeth with an envelope with her name on it terrified him into paralysis.

He removed the poem from his jacket pocket and held it in his hand. *So don't give it to her. If you're that upset about it, tear it up and throw it away,* said the sane, rational voice of his brain. *You wrote it, you got it out of your system, now chuck the stupid poem in the nearest garbage can.*

Tom stared down at the off-white envelope with Elizabeth Wakefield typed across the front. *You can't throw it away,* the insane, irrational voice of his heart said. *You just can't. Even if she laughs at you, even if she refuses to speak to you again, you have to try to make her understand. If you don't reach out for Elizabeth, you may never love anyone again.*

"So I guess I'm going to listen to my heart," Tom said as he started across the street. "I guess I'm on automatic *and* self-destruct."

Elizabeth looked up as the door burst open and Celine swooshed into the room. She'd been so sure that Celine wouldn't be back for hours that she couldn't hide a frown of disappointment.

"Don't get your pantyhose in a knot, princess," Celine said, noticing the frown. "I'm not staying." She dumped her books and several shopping bags on her bed. "I just want to change out of these grungy clothes. I've got a late date." She tossed an envelope onto the desk beside Elizabeth. "Here," Celine said, undoing her skirt and letting it drop to the floor.

Elizabeth looked down. "What's this?"

Celine tossed her blouse over a chair with a shrug. "How should I know? It was in our mailbox, and it has your name on it." She laughed sarcastically. "Maybe our perfect princess has a secret admirer. Stranger things have happened, haven't they?" She opened her closet.

"Yes," Elizabeth said sweetly. "*You* have admirers, after all."

"Oh, ha ha ha," Celine said. She pulled out something red and slinky and held it up to herself in front of the mirror. "Knowing you, it's probably just a note from the dorm monitor to thank you for always rinsing out the bathroom sink after you've used it."

Elizabeth scowled at Celine's back. The horrible truth was that Celine was probably right. It probably was a note from the dorm monitor, or someone like the dorm monitor. While Celine threw the red dress aside and pulled out something orange and made of Lycra, Elizabeth tore open the envelope.

It wasn't a note from the dorm monitor. Not at all. Elizabeth had to read the first stanza over several times before she understood what it was. It was a poem, a poem written for her.

Celine humphed and sighed and complained

about having nothing to wear as Elizabeth read the typed page in her hand with amazement. The poem was beautiful and poignant, and it moved her so much that she completely forgot she wasn't alone.

"What is that?" Celine's head appeared over her shoulder. "It looks like some kind of poem."

Elizabeth went to lay it facedown on the desk, but Celine was too fast. She snatched it out of her hand with a cry of delight. "It is!" she squealed. "Some poor deluded jerk is writing the princess poetry!"

"Give that back to me," Elizabeth ordered. "Or you really will have nothing to wear because I'll cut everything you own into tiny pieces."

"Be my guest." Celine opened her hand and let the poem float to the ground. "I'm certainly not interested in your pathetic love life." She slung her bag over her shoulder and banged out of the room.

As soon as she was sure Celine was gone, Elizabeth took the poem and sat on her bed to reread it. When she came to the end there was a catch in her voice as she read out loud, *"But I'm too afraid to try . . ."*

Elizabeth rested the page on her lap with a sigh. Who could have written such a beautiful piece of poetry? Who could have these feelings for her?

Tom. It was the first name that came into her head. The thought made her heart race. She picked up the poem again. Tom was an investigative reporter, not a poet, she reminded herself. He'd never shown any interest in poetry, not even when he'd seen the books she was reading.

She leaned back against her pillow. "Do you think it's Tom because it really might be Tom?" she wondered out loud. "Or is it because you want it to be him?"

Chapter
Ten

Steven came racing up the bleacher stairs with a cardboard tray filled with hot dogs, sodas, and popcorn. "This is the life!" he exclaimed as he sat down beside Billie. "A beautiful autumn day, a beautiful Homecoming game, and a beautiful woman to share them both with." He leaned over and kissed her. For today, at least, Steven had decided to put his concern for his sisters out of his mind and to have a good time.

"Never mind all that soppy stuff," Billie teased, kissing him back. "Unhand my frank."

Steven laughed, suddenly realizing that this was the most relaxed he'd felt in weeks. *Since the beginning of the term*, he told himself. *Since Elizabeth and Jessica arrived*. Steven sighed. The twins had been so cute and so much fun when they were little. He'd been the happiest big brother in the world. Now Elizabeth was lonely and miserable, and Jessica was spending far too much time with the cretin downstairs. It terrified him to think what either of them might do next.

Billie poked him with her elbow. "Stop it," she ordered.

"Stop what?" he asked innocently.

"Stop thinking about your sisters. You promised you wouldn't think about them all afternoon. You swore the only thing in your head would be football and me."

Steven grinned. "How did you know I was thinking about them?"

She gave him a wry smile. "Because you get the exact same look on your face my father used to get when I first started going out with boys."

"Well, Ms. Detective," Steven said. "It just might interest you to know that I wasn't really thinking about them. I was thinking how good it felt not to worry about them for a couple of hours."

"Well, stop thinking about it and just enjoy it. This is going to be a great game." She kissed his cheek.

"It's a great game already," Steven said, putting his arm around her. "And it hasn't even started yet."

He bit into his hot dog and gazed happily across the stands. It looked as though the entire school had turned out for it. He saw his sociology professor, three of his good friends from the prelaw program, Billie's friend Sandi and her boyfriend, and he saw Elizabeth and Peter Wilbourne.

The hot dog turned to sand in Steven's mouth. He gave Billie a shake. "Billie, look over there! Where those Thetas are sitting. Tell me what you see."

Billie followed the direction his hand was pointing. "I see Elizabeth and Peter Wilbourne."

Steven turned to her, disbelief on his face. "And that seems all right to you?"

Billie shrugged. "It seems a little strange. I thought Elizabeth didn't like Peter, but I guess she changed her mind."

"Billie," Steven said, fighting to remain calm. "Nobody with half a brain likes Peter. The guy's a power-happy bigot with an ego as big as Alaska."

She eyed him warily. "Oh, don't get started on him now, Steven. At least he doesn't drive a motorcycle and live in our building—that should make you happy."

"Well, it doesn't make me happy." He threw his hot dog back in the tray. "What is it with my sisters? Jessica's always been a little flaky, especially when it comes to boys, but Elizabeth was always rational. Elizabeth—"

"Steven!" Billie looked as if she was about to dump her soda over his head. "Stop it! When are you going to accept the fact that your sisters are adults now, and that they can go out whomever they want? They have to take responsibility for their own lives."

"I do accept that, Billie. It's just that—"

"The game's about to start, Steven. Let's just watch the game and have a good time, all right?"

"All right." He sat back. "Looks like they've got a good lineup this season, doesn't it?" he asked as the SVU Vanguards jogged onto the field.

Billie nodded. "It's amazing how Coach Sanchez has brought the team back after they lost Tom Watts, isn't it?" she asked.

"Yeah," Steven said. "He's really worked some miracles in the athletics department." But though his mouth was talking about football, he was still thinking about his sisters. *Jessica's with Mike McAllery, and Elizabeth is with Peter Wilbourne*, he thought miserably. *Maybe the twins are more identical than I thought. They both have really lousy taste in men.*

Tom shifted in his seat as the band came onto the field for half-time.

Danny looked over at him. "You ever miss it?" he asked.

Tom nodded. "Yeah. I don't regret giving it up, but I miss it all the time."

It wasn't the sport that he hadn't liked. He loved football. What he hadn't liked was the way being a superjock had made *him*—arrogant, thinking the world owed him a living. And what he hated was the fact that if he hadn't been so wound up in himself, his family would still be alive.

210

"Especially when we're getting massacred and I know I could've done something about it," Tom added with a small smile.

A raucous whoop went up from a group of Thetas and their dates a few rows below them.

"I wish someone could do something about them," Danny said, glancing down at them. "Football game, fraternity party, it's all the same to them."

Tom looked down the bleachers. "It's Wilbourne. You know he hates anything to take the attention away from him, even a Homecoming—" The word "game" died in Tom's throat as Peter Wilbourne and his date suddenly stood up in the center of their group.

"I don't believe it," Danny said. "It's Elizabeth Wakefield."

Tom couldn't take his eyes from the smiling couple. "You're sure that's Elizabeth?" he asked, laboring to keep his voice flat. "You went out with Jessica. Are you sure it's not her?"

Danny shook his head. "Look at the way she's dressed. Look at the way she moves. I'm sure that's not Jessica."

Tom's fingernails dug into the palms of his hands. What a jerk he was. What a fully paid-up member of the bozo club. He'd written her a poem! He'd poured his heart and soul out to her. He'd thought Elizabeth Wakefield was going to be the person to help him put his heart back together

211

again. What a joke! She wasn't interested in him. She was interested in Peter Wilbourne III. What an ass she must think he was. She'd probably laughed herself silly when she read his poem.

Even as Tom watched in horror, Elizabeth and Peter kissed. Right there in the middle of the stadium, for the entire school to see.

Laughed? She'd probably read it to Peter Wilbourne and the two of them had laughed together.

"I don't mind admitting when I've been wrong," the girl who looked, acted, and sounded exactly like Elizabeth Wakefield was saying in a loud, clear voice. "And I was wrong about you, Peter. I was very wrong, and I'm sorry." She took Peter Wilbourne's hand. "I'm really and truly sorry."

Isabella smiled to herself. She had to hand it to Jessica—she was so convincing as her twin that even Isabella could believe she was Elizabeth.

"I accept your apology," Peter said solemnly. "And I forgive you." He pulled her to him. "Let's kiss and make up. You know it's what you've wanted all along."

Pass me a barf bag, Isabella thought. *I'm going to be sick.* She turned away as Peter moved in for his kiss. What a jerk he was. What a complete and total jerk.

The group of Thetas and Sigmas whistled and cheered.

Isabella glanced behind her, searching for

something to look at that wouldn't make her feel ill. And there he was, looking amazingly handsome in a hooded sweatshirt and a pair of old jeans, staring intently down at them. Isabella's heart banged against her ribs. Had she been wrong in thinking that Tom Watts didn't know or care that she was alive? Could it be that Tom was watching her?

Isabella put her hand over her eyes as though shielding them from the sun and pretended to scan the crowd, but in reality she was studying Tom's face. His expression was more than intent—it was pained. He almost looked as though he'd seen a ghost.

It's not me he's looking at at all, Isabella realized with a pang. *It's Jessica!* She turned back to the Thetas and the truth hit her like a runaway train. It wasn't Jessica that Tom was watching with such hurt and longing. It was Elizabeth.

There was so much emotion in that expression. She was certain of it. *So Tom Watts isn't the complete loner everyone says*, Isabella thought as she gazed vacantly down at the field. *He is capable of love*. It was just unfortunate that it wasn't Isabella he was in love with.

After that kiss, it wasn't easy for Jessica to convince Peter Wilbourne that she didn't want to spend the rest of the afternoon with him. Thank God, he already had a date for the Homecoming dance or he would have expected her to go to that with him too. Jessica shuddered as she raced away after the game like Cinderella running out of the ball. She'd had about as much of Peter Wilbourne III as she could take for one lifetime. He had to be the most egotistical bore she'd ever met.

But all's well that ends well, Jessica told herself as she strode toward her dorm. *It was just like the dentist. You hate going, but when it's all over, you feel better.*

Alison had congratulated her as she was leaving on being pledged to the Thetas. "I can admit when I'm wrong too," Alison had said. "I think both you and Jessica will make terrific Thetas, and so does everyone else."

Jessica crossed the road to her hall. She didn't really smile, but the frown she'd been wearing since she discovered the truth about Mike faded a little. She'd probably never get over Mike, but at least she belonged to the best sorority in California. If she was going to have to learn to live with a broken heart, she'd rather do it as a Theta Alpha Theta than as a nobody.

Still thinking about Mike, Jessica entered her building. A group of girls she knew were in the lobby, making plans for the Homecoming dance that night. Jessica winced. She could have gotten another date for tonight if she'd really wanted to, but for the first time in her life she preferred just to stay home by herself. If she couldn't go with Mike, then she didn't want to go at all. Dancing and laughing with someone else wouldn't make her happy, it would smash another hole in her heart.

The lift she'd gotten from fooling the Thetas into pledging both her and Elizabeth vanished completely as Jessica climbed the stairs to her floor.

I guess the good news is that this is the worst I'll feel for as long as I live, she thought as she reached her landing.

It was just at that moment that she heard it. So quietly at first . . . *Love me tender, love me true . . .* Jessica's hand was on the door, but she couldn't open it. Someone on her floor was playing an old crackling Elvis Presley record. And it wasn't just any song; it was the song Mike had played the night he made love to her. It was *their* song. *For my darling, I love you . . .* Tears welled up in Jessica's eyes and her breath caught in a sob. No, she couldn't imagine ever feeling worse than this. . . . *And I always will.*

Overwhelmed with the need to be in her room where she could be alone and cry what was left of her heart out, Jessica stumbled into the hallway. The song ended and then, to her horror, started again. The tears spilled over her cheeks as she hurried around the corner to her room.

Suddenly she pulled to a stop. Her body froze.

Mike McAllery was sitting on the floor outside her room, leaning against the door, a boom box beside him. *Love me tender, love me true . . .*

She studied his face, her heart hammering in her chest. He looked haggard and ravaged, as though he hadn't slept or eaten in days, as though . . .

And suddenly she was struck by an astonishing thought. A thought that gave her a weak feeling in the bottom of her stomach. Mike looked as though he might have a broken heart too.

. . . And I always will.

Mike didn't move, but stared straight into her eyes and held them. "I love you, Jessica," he said softly. "I really love you." Very slowly he got to his feet. "Maybe you've got a right to be mad at me, but if you'd give me a chance, I know I can explain." He opened his arms. "Let me explain, Jess. Please . . ."

Over the roar of her heart she could hear Isabella telling her not to listen to Mike's excuses. She could hear Steven and Elizabeth telling her to run for her life. But Jessica didn't care. It didn't matter what they thought. It didn't matter about those other women. Nothing mattered except the fact that Mike loved her. He loved her, and he was sorry for hurting her. He loved her, and he was begging her to take him back.

Without a second's hesitation, she threw herself into his waiting arms.

Celine had flounced off to the bathroom to finish putting on her makeup, with a "Do try to make my Homecoming date feel comfortable if he arrives before I'm back, won't you, princess?"

Elizabeth had to stop herself from saying, *You mean he won't be in a cage?* But she didn't want to fight with Celine tonight. She was feeling much too miserable. She hadn't even been cheered up by the fact that this afternoon when she weighed herself, Nina's scale had claimed that she'd lost three pounds. As though it wasn't bad enough that everyone else in the world but her was going to the dance tonight, but this afternoon the Pi Beta Phis had let her know that they weren't accepting her pledge. The Pis thought Elizabeth was more Theta material. And there was something slightly weird and hinty about the way they said it. It was so ironic that if she hadn't been so disappointed by the rejection, she might have laughed.

When the knock came announcing the arrival of Celine's date, Elizabeth put down the book she was reading with a sigh. The last thing she needed was to have to make pleasant conversation with one of Celine's Neanderthal boyfriends.

She got up from her desk and opened the door. The man standing there with a corsage in his hand and a polite smile on his face might have just left a poetry reading, but he definitely hadn't been let out of a cage.

"You!" Elizabeth was so surprised to find herself staring into the handsome, enigmatic face of William White that she blurted out the first thing that came to her mind. "What are you doing here?"

His eyes went up and down her, taking in the twist of golden hair pinned up on her head and the old jeans and plaid flannel shirt she was wearing. He looked even more surprised than she felt. "And why aren't you dressed for the dance?" he asked. "Or is that what the real style-setters are wearing this year?"

Feeling, for some reason, as though she'd just been complimented, Elizabeth finally returned his smile. "I know this outfit would make a real fashion statement," she said, "but the truth is I'm not going."

"Not going?" He looked almost happy. "A beautiful girl like you isn't going to the Homecoming ball?"

Now she knew she'd been complimented. She shook her head. "I decided to skip the dance this year." She shrugged and her smile brightened a little. "I'd actually rather stay here and read Whitman."

He followed her into the room. "Whitman's overrated," he said, stopping at her desk and picking up the volume of poems she'd left there. "He's got some good stuff, but I've always felt he was a little too earnest. If you'd actually spent an evening with him, he would probably have turned out to be an awful bore."

"It's just as well he didn't ask me to the dance, then, isn't it?" Elizabeth joked.

William White turned from the book to her. "Who did ask you?"

As surprised by the question as by the fact that the intelligent and elegant William White had a date with Celine, Elizabeth again told the truth. "No one." She felt herself flush. "I guess the men at this school were afraid to go to Homecoming with a woman dressed for hiking."

There was a sudden gleam in those cool blue eyes. "I wouldn't have been afraid." His voice sounded unusually warm and gentle.

Her cheeks turned a deeper pink. As impossible as it seemed, William White was flirting with her. Before she could recover herself enough to respond, Celine sailed into the room in a cloud of perfume and washed silk.

"William!" she purred. "I am so sorry to have kept you waiting. I hope Elizabeth made you feel at home."

He looked over at Celine, but when he spoke all warmth and gentleness were gone. "That's not the only thing you have to be sorry for," he said.

"We're sorry to barge in like this," Billie said as she sat down on Elizabeth's bed. "But you know what these big dances are like. Steven was afraid we wouldn't even have a chance to say hello to you if we didn't stop by on our way."

Steven shoved some of Celine's things to one side and positioned himself gingerly on the edge of her desk.

"Don't apologize," Elizabeth answered sincerely. "It's really good to see you." Which was the truth. She was so rattled by her encounter with William White, she was glad for a dose of normalcy.

At least Billie was normal. She chatted happily about the evening ahead, asking Elizabeth what she thought about her hair and her dress and complaining that her shoes were too tight. Steven was not normal. Steven was looking at Elizabeth in a way that he usually reserved for Jessica: perplexed, frustrated, disappointed.

"Why aren't you dressed?" he asked when Billie's voice finally trailed off into silence. "Won't Peter Wilbourne be picking you up soon?"

Elizabeth's smile disappeared. "What?"

Steven was drumming his fingers on the desktop the way Mr. Wakefield did when he was upset about something. "You heard me," he said shortly. "You went to the game with Peter the Geek. Considering the way you were kissing him right there in broad daylight, I assumed you'd be going to the dance with him too."

Elizabeth could feel something going very wrong with her blood. It was turning to ice. "What?" she whispered.

Billie stood up. "Steven, you promised . . ."

Steven stood up too, refusing even to glance at Billie. "Come on, Liz. We saw you. Practically the whole school saw you." He shook his head. "After the way he treated you and Jess— I just can't *believe* you'd go out with a creep like that."

220

Billie's voice was sharp. "Steven—"

Elizabeth cut her off. "What are you talking about? I wouldn't go out with Peter Wilbourne if he was the last man on earth. I've been in this room the entire day."

Steven stared at her. Elizabeth stared back. The truth hit them both at exactly the same moment.

"Jessica!"

Billie let out her breath. "What a relief," she said, slipping her arm into Steven's. "Your brother's been driving me crazy because he thought you were going out with Peter."

Elizabeth wasn't relieved. She was furious. Of all the low-down, sneaky things her twin had done to her in the last eighteen years, this had to be the worst. Knowing how strongly Elizabeth felt about Peter, Jessica had gone ahead and impersonated her just so she could get into some obnoxious, stuck-up sorority.

"Elizabeth?" Steven said. Both he and Billie were looking at her with concern. "Are you okay? You look like you're about to explode."

Elizabeth's eyes were flashing and her jaw was set. "I am about to explode," she said. "I can't believe she did that to me. After I told her I wouldn't go out with him, not under any circumstances, no matter what the stupid Thetas wanted—" She broke off, too furious to go on.

Steven came over and put a hand on her shoulder. "I'll talk to her, Liz. Jessica's been getting

221

pretty carried away with herself lately. I want to try to reason with her if I can."

Suddenly Billie was standing beside him. "Why can't you let them work out their own problems?" she demanded. She picked up her bag from Elizabeth's desk. "Why do you have to interfere all the time?"

"Billie's right," Elizabeth said quickly. She didn't want Steven talking to Jessica. She wanted to wring Jessica's neck herself. "I'll handle Jess. Believe me, I know exactly what I want to say."

How could she have doubted Mike for even a few minutes? Jessica wondered as he opened the door to the Corvette and took her hand. He looked wonderful in his dark Italian suit. He *was* wonderful. After she'd given him a chance to explain, she'd realized that.

He hadn't been cheating on her with the woman in the Karmann Ghia. He'd been negotiating to buy the car for Jessica and fix it up.

Isabella was wrong. Mike wasn't into any shady dealings; Mike bought old cars and fixed them up. That's how he made money. That was what he'd done with his Corvette. That was what he was going to do with Whatever-her-name-was's Karmann Ghia.

"I love you," he whispered as she stepped out of the car and into his arms. "I've never said that to anybody before, Jess." He cupped her chin in his hands and gazed into her eyes. "I've never said it, because I never felt it."

Jessica felt more beautiful than she ever had before standing there with him on the sidewalk. Her golden hair was up in a twist, her neck and shoulders left bare by her long, strapless, fitted red dress.

"I love you, too," Jessica whispered back. "And I'm sorry I acted like such a jealous child. I—"

He put a finger to her lips. "Let's not talk about it anymore. Let's just forget it ever happened."

"Forget what happened?" she asked with a laugh.

Enid Rollins was so happy she couldn't stop smiling. She'd smiled all through the game this afternoon, sitting on the bleachers with Mark's arm around her, only half aware of what was happening on the field. She'd smiled all through the exquisite meal at Da Vinci's with Todd and Lauren. She'd smiled all the way back to campus in Mark's new Explorer, so happy that it didn't bother her even a little that the guys did nothing but talk about football the entire way. And she was smiling now as the four of them strolled through the warm night to the Homecoming ball.

"Someone may have to pinch me," she said with a laugh. "This day has been so unbelievably great I feel like I'm dreaming."

"Somebody better pinch me, too," Todd said from behind her. "I think the dream just turned into a nightmare."

Mark, Enid, and Lauren all saw what he was talking about at the same time, and they all stopped suddenly. Coming toward them in a direct line across their path was Elizabeth Wakefield. She had a sweater thrown over an old shirt and jeans, and she was moving fast. She looked upset.

"Elizabeth!" Enid said.

Elizabeth came to a halt. It was clear from the expression on her face that she hadn't seen them until this moment. Her eyes moved from Enid to Todd, and then to Lauren and Mark. They settled back on Enid as she forced something that was almost a smile onto her face.

For a second, Enid was afraid that none of them were going to be able to speak, that they were just going to stand there in an awkward silence for the rest of their lives. She tried desperately to think of something to say. But what? *We just had a wonderful dinner? Don't you think Todd looks handsome in his dinner jacket? My, but those jeans are very becoming on you, Liz?* Beside her, the guys cleared their throats, but no words came out.

It was Elizabeth who finally thought of something to say. "You look great, Alexandra," she said. in a voice that was barely more than a whisper. "You look really great."

Enid smiled back. "Thanks," she said. "I—you—" She broke off, unable to continue.

Mark came to her rescue. "Why aren't you dressed up?" he said to Elizabeth. "Isn't Peter

Wilbourne taking you to the ball?"

Elizabeth looked as though he'd slapped her. Without any answer, she rushed away.

"Wow," Todd said as soon as Elizabeth was out of earshot. "That was unpleasant."

"Well, it's over now," Lauren said. "Let's just pretend that it didn't happen and go back to having a good time."

Enid pushed the memory of Elizabeth's stricken face from her mind. "Lauren's right," she said brightly. "This is a perfect day. Let's not let anything spoil it."

Winston tiptoed down the corridor, his arms filled with bags of chips and a two-liter bottle of soda, afraid to disturb the unearthly quiet of Oakley Hall.

"I feel like the last of the Mohicans," Winston mumbled to himself as he walked toward the common room.

"It's too bad I don't feel like studying," he continued. "It's the one night I could actually work without being disturbed by someone in a hair crisis or having a fight with her boyfriend."

But Winston didn't feel like studying. He felt like watching two or three really awful horror movies on the TV and eating himself into a coma on nachos and potato chips.

He shoved the common-room door open so hard that it banged against the wall.

"I can't believe it," Winston grumbled as he threw his things on the counter and fished through the stuff on the table for the TV guide. "My first college Homecoming ball and I'm not at it."

"Well, why aren't you?"

Winston caught his breath, not daring to turn around. There was no one else in the room. If there were, he would have seen them when he came in. *Good grief,* he thought, *this is what they've driven me to. I'm finally cracking up. I'm hearing voices.*

There was a ripple of laughter that sounded just like tiny silver bells.

Winston recognized that laugh. He turned around.

Denise was leaning over the back of the couch, grinning at him. "So why didn't you go?" she asked again. She smiled. "Don't tell me you were struck by the curse of the Sigmas and couldn't get a date."

He returned her grin. "It was more that I was afraid I'd be struck by the Sigmas themselves if I turned up with a date when they'd all been stood up," Winston confessed. Which was half the truth. The other half was vaulting over the couch, coming to see what food he had. He hadn't had the nerve to ask Denise, and she was the only girl he really wanted to go with.

"You're right," Denise said, stopping so close beside him that he could smell the shampoo she'd just used to wash her hair. It was papaya. "They probably would have."

"What about you?" Winston asked. "Don't tell me you're not feeling well again?"

"Yum, salt-and-vinegar potato chips," Denise said. "My favorite." She tore herself away from the chips and gave him a smile. "No, I feel fine. I just didn't feel like going to the ball with Bill, and he's the only one who asked me."

Winston could hardly hide his surprise. "The only one?"

She shrugged. "Okay, one of the only ones. But I didn't want to go with any of the others, either. I thought I'd have more fun if I stayed here and washed my hair." She picked up the bag of her favorite potato chips. "And it looks like I was right."

Winston didn't trust himself to speak. The dorm was empty, the night was young, and he and Denise Waters were alone together with half-a-dozen bags of snack food and a two-liter bottle of soda. He must be cracking up. He wasn't only hearing voices, he was having hallucinations.

"So, Win," Denise said, shaking the television guide he was still holding in his hands. "What are we watching?"

Winston scooped up the chips and soda and followed her to the couch. "Well, there's a horror double-feature on that I was going to watch," he said hesitantly. "*Revenge of the Lost Corpse* and *Assassins from the Forbidden Planet*. But we could watch something else, if you want."

Denise handed him the remote. "Are you kidding? *Assassins from the Forbidden Planet* is one of my all-time favorite movies. It's a classic."

He plopped down beside her, unable to believe the strange ways things happened. Five minutes ago he was facing one of the worst nights of his life. And now . . . *Assassins from the Forbidden Planet* and Denise Waters not two feet away from him.

"I'm so glad you didn't go to the dance, Win," Denise said. "I don't mind admitting that I was already feeling bored." She opened the bag of salt-and-vinegar potato chips. "But this is going to be really great. This is my idea of a perfect evening."

"Mine, too," Winston said, sinking into a state of bliss.

Elizabeth found herself walking almost blindly toward the TV station. She'd started out on a mission to find Jessica and have it out with her. And then, of course, she'd run into Alexandra and Todd. She felt the deep ache in her throat of tears about to come. She couldn't decide which was worse: seeing them all so dressed up and happy or discovering they thought she was dating Peter Wilbourne.

But Elizabeth was beyond caring. She didn't want to go back to the dorm, she didn't want to go anywhere there were bright lights and people. She wanted someplace she felt safe, where she could try to piece her heart back together again. And that place was Tom's office at WSVU. Tom wouldn't be there. He was probably at the ball with Isabella Ricci.

Which is better anyway, Elizabeth told herself as she slipped into the building. *I don't want him to be here. I just want to be alone. I don't want anything from anyone ever again.* She hurried down the corridor as a new wave of crying threatened to overtake her. *He won't be here, so it doesn't matter. But even if he were here, I wouldn't want him to be. Even if he did write that poem, I don't want him to be here. Even if* . . . her thoughts trailed off as she stepped into the office.

A light was on over the desk in the corner, and a figure was stooped over the desk.

Tom was there. Of course he was. And maybe she did want him to be there. Because she found herself fighting the most desperate urge to run to him. To throw herself in his arms and stay there forever.

Once again her mind turned back to the poem. The beautiful lines that made her eyes fill with tears. *Was it you, Tom?* She needed to know. She stepped silently toward him, unsure of what she was doing, carried by her heart.

Suddenly Tom turned around. His eyes locked on hers. She found herself frantically searching his face for the love and the tenderness she so desperately needed right now.

It wasn't there. She could see that immediately. The hardness in his eyes made her entire body freeze.

Tom turned his eyes from hers. "What are you doing here?" he asked coldly.

She'd been wrong. She wasn't safe here. And she'd been wrong about the poem. Tom hadn't written it. No one could have written those things and be looking at her now with such iciness, such detachment. Why had she let herself believe it could have been him? For the second time that night, Elizabeth turned and fled without a word.

She was halfway down the hall when she heard him running after her. "Elizabeth!" he shouted. "Elizabeth! Wait! I'm sorry—I—Elizabeth!"

Not as sorry as I am, Elizabeth thought.

She'd find no love here. It was time to accept that. The tears began to fall again as she reached the front doors and hurled herself into the black night. *Not as sorry as I am.*

Jessica felt as though she were floating on air as they entered the crowded hall, hand in hand. Hundreds of balloons in autumn colors shaded the lights and cascaded from the ceiling. The band stood on a stage lit by candles.

This is so perfect, so absolutely perfect, Jessica thought as she held Mike tight and looked around. *It's a perfect evening. I have the perfect boyfriend. I belong to the perfect sorority . . .* A feeling of joy bubbled through her. *My life is absolutely perfect.*

She could feel the eyes on them as they crossed the room. No one could deny that she and Mike were a stunning couple. Jessica smiled to herself. Peter Wilbourne III definitely looked stunned. Jessica flashed him her smuggest smile. Out of the corner of her eye she saw Isabella, standing to one side with Alison Quinn. Isabella looked pretty stunned too. Stunned and outraged. Jessica sighed to herself. At some point soon she was going to have to face Isabella and another lecture.

But not right now, she told herself as Mike took her in his arms and they began to dance. *Right now I just want to enjoy being the happiest girl in the world.*

"So tell me, Jess," Mike whispered as he pulled her close. "Will you move in with me?" He touched his lips to her hair. "If you live with me, you'll never have to be jealous again."

Jessica closed her eyes and leaned against his strong, hard chest. "Yes," she said, her heart soaring. "I'd love to."

And I'm going to be the happiest girl in the world for the rest of my life.

We hope you enjoyed reading this book. If you would like to receive further information about available titles in the Bantam series, just write to the following address, with your name and address: Kim Prior, Bantam Books, 61–63 Uxbridge Road, Ealing, London W5 5SA.

If you live in Australia or New Zealand and would like more information about the series, please write to:

Sally Porter
Transworld Publishers
(Australia) Pty Ltd
15–25 Helles Avenue
Moorebank
NSW 2170
AUSTRALIA

Kiri Martin
Transworld Publishers (NZ) Ltd
3 William Pickering Drive
Albany
Auckland
NEW ZEALAND

SWEET VALLEY HIGH

The top-selling teenage series starring identical twins Jessica and Elizabeth Wakefield and all their friends at Sweet Valley High. One new title every month!

1. DOUBLE LOVE
2. SECRETS
3. PLAYING WITH FIRE
4. POWER PLAY
5. ALL NIGHT LONG
6. DANGEROUS LOVE
7. DEAR SISTER
8. HEARTBREAKER
9. RACING HEARTS
10. WRONG KIND OF GIRL
11. TOO GOOD TO BE TRUE
13. KIDNAPPED
14. DECEPTIONS
15. PROMISES
16. RAGS TO RICHES
17. LOVE LETTERS
18. HEAD OVER HEELS
19. SHOWDOWN
20. CRASH LANDING
23. SAY GOODBYE
24. MEMORIES
26. HOSTAGE
27. LOVESTRUCK
29. BITTER RIVALS
30. JEALOUS LIES
35. OUT OF CONTROL
36. LAST CHANCE
44. PRETENCES
54. TWO-BOY WEEKEND
63. THE NEW ELIZABETH

67. THE PARENT PLOT
69. FRIEND AGAINST FRIEND
70. MS QUARTERBACK
71. STARRING JESSICA
72. ROCK STAR'S GIRL
74. THE PERFECT GIRL
75. AMY'S TRUE LOVE
76. MISS TEEN SWEET VALLEY
77. CHEATING TO WIN
78. THE DATING GAME
79. THE LONG-LOST BROTHER
80. THE GIRL THEY BOTH
      LOVED
81. ROSA'S LIE
82. KIDNAPPED BY THE CULT!
83. STEVEN'S BRIDE
84. THE STOLEN DIARY
86. JESSICA AGAINST BRUCE
87. MY BEST FRIEND'S
      BOYFRIEND
88. LOVE LETTERS FOR SALE
89. ELIZABETH BETRAYED
90. DON'T GO HOME WITH
      JOHN
91. IN LOVE WITH A PRINCE
92. SHE'S NOT WHAT SHE
      SEEMS
93. STEPSISTERS
94. ARE WE IN LOVE?

Prom Thriller Mini-Series
Thriller: A NIGHT TO
     REMEMBER
95. THE MORNING AFTER
96. THE ARREST
97. THE VERDICT
98. THE WEDDING
99. BEWARE THE BABYSITTER
100. THE EVIL TWIN

Romance Trilogy
101. THE BOYFRIEND WAR
102. ALMOST MARRIED
103. OPERATION LOVE MATCH

Horror in London Mini-series
104. LOVE AND DEATH IN
     LONDON
105. A DATE WITH A
     WEREWOLF
106. BEWARE THE WOLFMAN

The Love and Lies Mini-series
107. JESSICA'S SECRET LOVE

18 PINE STREET

THE PLACE TO BE!

18 PINE STREET is the hot new hangout where Sarah Gordon, her cousin Tasha, Cindy Phillips, Kwame Brown, April Winter, Dave Hunter and Jennifer Wilson meet to talk about their friends, dating – and life at Murphy High.

Look out for the following titles in this great new multicultural series by Walter Dean Myers – available in all good bookshops!

1. SORT OF SISTERS
2. THE PARTY
3. THE PRINCE
4. THE TEST
5. SKY MAN
6. FASHION BY TASHA